I0746431

BY THE SAME AUTHOR:

BATRIX & SCILLI ADVENTURES
Hail the New Age
Citadel of the Moon

DAMIAN PALADIN ADVENTURES
The Paladin Mandates
Walkers in Shadow

USS OSWIN
Drawing Down Leviathan

ARIEH QUARREL
Revenge Is A Cold Pistol

COLLECTIONS
Give Me These Moments Back
Radix Omnium Malum and Other Intruders

WARRIORS OF THE BOUNDLESS

MIKE CHINN

ILLUSTRATED BY

ENRIQUE ALCATENA

WITH AN INTRODUCTION BY

ADRIAN COLE

WARRIORS OF THE BOUNDLESS

Copyright © Mike Chinn 2025
Cover and interior artwork © Enrique Alcatena 2025
Introduction © Adrian Cole 2025

Published 2025 by Saladoth Productions by arrangement with the author. All rights reserved by the author. The right of Mike Chinn to be identified as the Author of this Work has been asserted by him in accordance with the Copyright, Design and Patents Act 1988.
No part of this publication may be reproduced, stored in a retrieval system or transmitted in any form or by any means, electronic, mechanical, photocopying, recording or otherwise, without prior permission of the copyright holder

FIRST EDITION

ISBN
978-1-7390938-2-2

"The Essence of Dust" was first published in SWORDS & SORCERIES 2 2021
"The Rains of Barofonn" was first published in SWORDS & SORCERIES 3, 2021
"Where the Sun Has Never Shone" was first published in
FANTASY TALES Vol.12 #6 1991 as "Day of the Dark Men"
"The Airs of Eden" was first published in SWORDS & HEROES online, 2023
All of the above have been revised for this publication

"The Power of the Serpent" and "Hand of Glory" are original to this publication

The Voidal appears by kind permission of Adrian Cole

This book is a work of fiction. Names, characters, places and incidents are either products of the author's imagination or used fictitiously. Any resemblance to actual events or locales or persons, living or dead, is entirely coincidental.

Printed and bound by IngramSpark

SALADOTH PRODUCTIONS

Hall Green, Birmingham
United Kingdom

*My thanks to Adrian Cole
for agreeing to write the introduction to this volume,
and for letting me play in part of his sandbox for a while;
to Quique Alcatena for the gorgeous cover and interior
illustrations, which bring back so many memories of our time
working together on DC Thomson's Starblazer comic;
and also to Lyndon Perry for his editing work.*

*This book is dedicated to Michael Moorcock,
whose 1969 edition of Stormbringer
– a Christmas present from a friend who knew not what he did –
would eventually set me off on a Moonbeam Road of my own.*

TABLE OF CONTENTS

INTRODUCTION: LET SLIP THE DOGS OF ... WILD IMAGINATION

APPARENTLY SWORD AND sorcery is currently enjoying a major revival, as a new pulp era grows and spawns a wave of material to rival the golden age of the 1970s, when the masters of the Sword and Sorcery art conquered a world hungry for its imaginative sweep. I say apparently because, although there are as many people currently writing Sword and Sorcery as there are pebbles on my local beach (Westward Ho! UK in Solomon Kane country) the genre is not breaking sales records. Far from it, according to publishers and editors I communicate with.

But it's definitely on the up and up. And here's the proof that among those pebbles there are jewels to be found. *Warriors of the Boundless* is one such. Mike Chinn's fascinating story clearly draws inspiration from Sword and Sorcery masters of the past, notably Michael Moorcock, Jack Vance and Clark Ashton Smith, to name but three. Add to that more than a pinch of superhero related world building and a fusion of magic and warped technology and you have a hugely entertaining concoction.

The writing is very polished, the product of long years of development, the quality of the style contributing a powerful dimension to the narrative. Here there is carefully worded use of language, power in the writing without making it overwhelming. There is action aplenty, enough blood and gore to assuage the thirst of any Sword and Sorcery aficionad; although, satisfyingly, the prose does not bludgeon.

Among the diverse and intriguing characters, the Voidal (the haunted, god-cursed dark man of my own saga) steps out of his personal ongoing predicament to weave an equally obtuse course herein. However, this is an alternative Voidal, more terrified than terrifying and even more humbled and diminished by the vicissitudes of these experiences. Mike Chinn's version exists in a very different though equally tormented universe. Perhaps the entire episode is a wild sequence of dreams, sent to the Voidal by the Dark Gods in another of their efforts to deflect him from his determination to thwart whatever destiny they have contrived for their own satisfaction. The confusion is apt, for in *Warriors of the Boundless* Mike Chinn has created a sequence of interlinking puzzles and conundrums in a delightful blaze of colour, a maze at the centre of which lies a suitably beguiling climax.

And if that isn't more than enough, the book is beautifully illustrated by Enrique Alcatena (who brought several of Mike's *Starblazer* comic scripts to life, back in the day), whose uniquely individual black and white pictures delve deep into the mystique of the stories, from the outrageous to the disturbing. Here is a neatly grafted partnership, a natural fusion of imaginations.

This is a book to be savoured, not gorged. But a feast, no less.

Adrian Cole
April 2025

12

THE OLD MAN, who was neither old nor a man, sank deep into his ritual. His body relaxed against a tall chair as his mind rose. Reaching out, his spirit expanded through Space, Time and the complex, infinite Tiers of the Internection. The Boundless. It had almost as many names as there were realities. Pasts and futures streamed past him in a chaotic blur that defied his understanding; a reckless stack of possibilities squirmed and wriggled free of his observation. Piercing the chaotic veils which screened Tier from Tier was a skill that had so far manifested in him only as random, untrustworthy glimpses. Eventually he hoped to be able to perceive the entire Boundless in a single, all-encompassing instant – every Tier, past, present and future (inasmuch as those terms meant anything across the swirling randomness that was the Internection). It was said only the gods could manage such a feat, and he was far from a god. Nevertheless, still he practised.

And so, by infinitesimal degrees, his abilities were honed.

He first sensed it as a misplaced note among the spheres' music, a sour taste in the mouth of his motionless, corporeal body. Something was wrong; wrong beyond the power of language. The Internection was compromised. Although the Infinite Tiers contained all possibilities, even including that of its own non-reality, sometimes those possibilities were kept at length, the paradox too great even for what was essentially an endless web of contradictions. Quarantined. And now something from those excluded regions had found access. Something from a reality beyond reality. Somewhen beyond his untrustworthy vision a Tier was injured, and infection had crept in. An invading body that the Internection, as an entity, was powerless to reject – in either the past, present or uncertain future.

Yet even as his mind detected the contagion, he also sensed the Boundless rallying its defences. Felt its call. Human and non-human, directed towards the wound. Some unknowing, some all too aware of their role.

He sighed. Among the many disparate sentient beings who thronged the Tiers – mortal and immortal – he had something of a reputation. Perhaps deserved, perhaps not. A dilettante; a meddler. One who, more often than they should, concerned themselves with matters perhaps best left to the gods, their messengers, or those who – with admirable dispassion – served the Boundless itself. They would likely distrust him as a matter of principle, doubt his word. He must be subtle.

And so, laying his plans carefully, he surrendered to his part.

15

THE ESSENCE OF DUST

DAS EWAN TOOK an uncoordinated step, pausing to steady himself against a nearby wall. It sagged under his weight and he almost fell. From behind him he heard a snigger and Ewan turned carefully. There was no one, just another swirl of grit on the cold night air, glittering in the light of the twin moons.

He frowned. Surely Tallach had been standing there? The man had been trailing him all the way back from the ramshackle drinking den, pleading with Ewan to share the wineskin they had pooled their last coppers to buy. And now he had wandered off, though Ewan could not imagine where. The outskirts of Caerbanth held nothing but empty, skeletal buildings as its citizens gradually retreated to the relatively intact centre. The lane was narrow, the flanking buildings all leaning precariously overhead, and there was no other street or alley leading off.

After a moment Ewan shook his head, reaching for the wineskin dangling off his belt. "Your loss, my friend." He raised the wineskin to his lips, but nothing came out. He upended it, frowning. Empty but for the sour bouquet of old wine. How was that possible? He brought the spout up to one eye, as though the act of looking could summon up a fresh reserve. Nothing.

Ewan hunched his broad shoulders in misery and stared hard up and down the moonlit lane. The grainy mists which perpetually filled Caerbanth's streets ebbed and flowed, occasionally obscuring his vision. A section of overhanging building fell, crumbling to dust before it reached the rotting cobbles. Ewan spat grit from a drying mouth and threw the wineskin aside.

He drew a ragged leather cloak around his gaunt body. He almost fell, legs organising themselves at the last moment. Locking his knees, he took a breath and resumed his unsteady trek, heading for what had once been a fine mansion at the foot of the mountains looming over the city: the manse of the Thane of Caerbanth. If Feruman was in a good mood maybe his old master would furnish Ewan with a drink or two, to see him through to the morning.

The lane ended abruptly, opening out onto a bleak, stony rise, stark in the moons' light. Nothing grew on these slopes; Ewan could not remember if anything ever had. Ahead was the mansion. Its ancient walls stood out so harsh and white in the moonlight it was almost possible for Ewan to ignore the pockmarks and network of cracks disfiguring them. Fool himself it wasn't as decayed as the rest of Caerbanth. Behind it reared the mountains, black and unforgiving. Ewan tried to keep his eyes averted from the vast, blurred shape growing on the higher slopes, like a huge fungus. It seemed to glow, daring him to look. Ewan stared instead at the nearing gates, concentrating on them.

Unsteadily, he pushed his way through thick wooden gates which felt as insubstantial as a spider's web. Beyond was a garden, choked with rubble and the gaunt remains of what once had been fragrant bushes. Back when the mansion had been more than an empty stone and brick shell, and titles mattered. When Feruman was Thane, and Ewan his Swordmaster. A lot of wine had flowed since then. Decent wine. Not the piss that was all Ewan could afford – even if better had been available. Which he knew, from experience, it wasn't.

"Feruman?" He stepped under a sagging veranda and pushed open the double doors leading into the echoing shell of a reception area: once richly-carved, now colourless and scarred by mildew. He flopped onto the bottom step of an ancient, dusty staircase. At his back was a rotting plastered wall.

"Feruman? Where are you, my ex and gracious lord?" The once Thane had taken to hiding away any drink, just in case Ewan stopped by. Even though the mansion was nothing but bare walls and tattered roof, with barely a stick of furniture, Feruman had grown inventive. Ewan didn't feel like a treasure hunt.

"Feruman! You bastard!"

He stood, hanging onto a banister even more unsteady than he, and made his way to the deserted banqueting hall. A sullen fire, signally failing to warm the empty space, burned at one end. Smoke curled out of the fireplace, masking the overall smell of rot. Diffident flames flickered around stacked kindling – the remains of some chair or other – reluctant to take hold. Ewan spat at it. He missed.

"Feruman!" Where in hell was he?

A diffuse, cold blue glow was attempting to make its way through the tall windows lining the outer wall, but could not pass through the filthy glass that seemed to droop with fatigue. The sun was rising, licking at Caerbanth with tired rays. Surely it wasn't morning already? What had happened to the night?

There was a long, scarred table standing haphazardly in the centre of the hall, the last of five magnificent boards which had once groaned with the finest food and drink. Four carver chairs lay nearby, so far spared the fire. Ewan hauled one upright and dropped into it.

He rubbed at his lined face. He licked parched lips. Wherever his ex-master was, Ewan hoped he would return with a drink. Feruman's rank, no matter how illusory, still meant something in certain quarters. He might acquire a half-decent skin or two, if he had a mind. Ewan ran a hand through his thin, greying hair, his face twisting into a self-pitying grin. As if it mattered anymore.

On the wall facing the fireplace hung a skeleton clock, as tall as Ewan had stood in his proud youth. Once it had marked time with commendable accuracy, looming over the high table, marking off each second of Thane Feruman's rule. Now it was lifeless. The mechanism appeared undamaged, yet no amount of winding or adjustment had coaxed the device into action.

Ewan was unsure why Feruman hadn't sold the thing for precious coin, or tossed it onto the fire before now – the frame was mostly wood, after all. Misplaced sentiment, he supposed.

He heard the squeal of the mansion's doors, the pad of footsteps. Ewan half rose, hands fumbling for a sword he had long ago exchanged for drink. A moment later the thin, weasel-faced Feruman limped into the hall. He spread himself in front of the fireplace, holding out naked hands for the meagre warmth. His ragged clothes bore no hint of the fine velvets and silks they had once been. Like so much else they were drab, colourless and spent. The cockscomb of his chaperon hat was stiff with grease.

Ewan sagged back into the chair. "Where have you been?" He sounded petulant. He didn't care. Feruman could hardly dismiss his services.

The other man was about to speak when another voice overrode him. "With me."

A figure stepped gracefully into the hall, stooping to pass through the doors: a woman, unnaturally tall, and dressed in loose black clothing. Ewan was about to thank Feruman for sharing his good fortune when the words died, unspoken. There was something about the newcomer, something ... wrong. Was she even a woman? Ewan had certainly never seen one quite like her before.

Oddly-hued, pale red hair fell to her shoulders; almond-shaped, ivy green eyes were set above sharp cheekbones. Her long face was pallid, almost white, with full, sensuous lips. Her features were exquisite. Ewan thought her ears, mostly hidden under the long hair, were sharp and narrow, although he could be imagining it. He imagined many things lately.

Despite the outside chill she wore no cloak, instead a long sword was sheathed across her back. Her left arm was encased in a silvery metal to the elbow. The surface seemed to flow like quicksilver, yet was etched in unrecognisable figures. Instead of a hand, two ornate claws flexed at its tip.

A black creature which might have been a huge cat, save for a face which looked far too human, slunk through the doorway. It crouched at the tall figure's feet, watchful grey eyes peering from its strange features.

"I am Uryell." The woman's voice was deep, melodious, her accent odd. She spoke Gjoranese awkwardly. A foreigner? Why would anyone from beyond Gjoran visit the place, especially Caerbanth?

Ewan stared at both the tall figure and the bizarre creature at her feet. "How may we assist you? Please forgive the sparsity of our abode. We are temporarily out of funds."

The newcomer swept cold eyes around the bare hall. "So I see. Perhaps I may be able to help your ... situation."

"You are generous. Do you have a full purse?"

Feruman hissed something Ewan didn't catch. Most likely annoyed that Ewan was taking it upon himself to interrogate the stranger. Well, what of it?

Uryell's lips curved into a warm smile. One which, Ewan noticed, did not reach her eyes. "No. Although I may be able to fill yours, if you have a mind."

Ewan tried to sneer. "And how do you intend to do that?"

"By raiding the citadel you call Cahercrioch."

For a moment Ewan was struck silent, before finding the mockery which seemed appropriate. "Then pray don't let us detain you. There's a path up the mountainside – the barbican's right there." He waved a hand vaguely.

"I am aware of the stronghold's location. Also its bearing on the fate of Caerbanth in particular, and your land of Gjoran in general." Uryell paused, as though considering her words. "As well as worlds beyond this moribund one."

She moved closer to the hearth. The flames' sullen glow was absorbed into her black frame, giving back no reflection. The temperature seemed to drop further. Sprawling on its side, the cat creature swept its cold gaze across Feruman and Ewan. Its too human features appeared to be laughing at them.

Ewan fidgeted on the stool. Damn, he needed a drink! "Sorry, whoever you are, my mind is presently not elevated enough to understand you. But furnish me with decent wine – or even a few breakfast ales, now the sun is risen – and I will presently match your nonsense phrase for phrase."

Uryell stared back at him. Ewan downcast his own eyes, unable to look at her strange beauty. "Spare me your judgement," he mumbled. "It is not I who blithely speaks of entering hell."

She shrugged. "As you will. I had merely thought to include you in the spoils, that is all."

"Spoils?" Ewan raised his head. He blinked at Uryell, then Feruman. "What spoils?"

"Listen." Feruman finally spoke. His voice was thin, and more ingratiating than usual. "Uryell has an interesting proposition."

"If it means I get a drink, I'm all ears." Ewan leaned back in his chair and stretched tired legs. "Propose on."

Uryell picked up another chair and folded herself into it. "It is my understanding the masters of Cahercrioch – the Chulainn – conquered Gjoran five centuries ago, built their fortress, and created a vassal state."

Feruman nodded. Ewan wanted to spit, but his mouth was drier than the gritty mists outside. "Common knowledge. And?"

"And then they disappeared, leaving Cahercrioch desolate – and likely filled with Gjoran's looted treasure."

Again, both men agreed. What, thought Ewan, was the point in going over Cahercrioch's bleak history? "Everyone knows they left behind vast wealth!" He was defensive, angry. "Why else should the castle's guardians still be there?"

"Why indeed." Uryell's grin widened. "I will be frank with you. If the Chulainn hoarded anything from their pillage of your world, it is of no interest to me. You may take it to redistribute, or keep for yourselves. What I seek is more than just gold and jewels."

What, wondered Ewan, could be more than that? "Why?"

Uryell leaned back a fraction, strange eyes half-lidded. "It must be stilled. This wretched town, your entire land, will continue to die by degrees if Cahercrioch is not shut down." Her smile grew wider still. Ewan thought it predatory. "Who knows, perhaps Gjoran will hail you both as its saviours once the citadel's influence is quelled and your world can once again ascend to normality."

Ewan licked parched lips, glancing briefly at Feruman. He did not need to ask the older man's opinion: the ex-Thane's rheumy eyes burned with fever. Was it the thought of celebrity, or the possibility of gold? Feruman had never been averse to either.

Ewan glanced through the window at the diffuse, pale blue orb just visible through it. Legend claimed, before the masters of Cahercrioch came, that weak sun had been a fiery ball, one which could blind any man who stared into its face. "Can we do it?" he wondered aloud.

"The four of us will." Clearly Uryell included her odd pet. "Cahercrioch's defences grow weak as its *velanke'en* ages. It will not be easy, but not insurmountable."

Velanke'en? he thought. What in hell's creation was a *velanke'en*? He began to wonder if the newcomer wasn't, after all, mad.

Ewan shared a glance with Feruman. They were thinking the same: to venture into Cahercrioch and steal the wealth therein. It was something they had often boasted of attempting whilst deep in their cups, and never considered when sober.

But with this Uryell? A woman, and quite probably mad...?

Ewan knew his mind was already made up. "Thane Feruman and I are embarrassingly short of arms."

Uryell's smile quirked. "Arms and armour can be provided."

"Then we are your men, Lady Uryell, provided—"

"You require payment in advance?"

Ewan made an expansive, generous gesture. "Not at all, but breakfast would be welcome."

Uryell came to her feet in a fluid motion. "Forgive me, gentlemen. One moment, if you please." She left the hall. Ewan heard the sound of footsteps fade into the desolate garden.

Ewan leaned forward. "Where did you find ... her?" he hissed.

Feruman gave him an odd look. "He found me."

"He?" Clearly the other man was drunker than Ewan. Or perhaps he saw what he wished to see – Feruman had always been partial to pretty boys. "That face! The voice! I don't know whether to fight her or fuck her—!" He fell silent as Uryell returned to the hall, dragging two bulging sacks. They chinked suggestively.

"Please. Help yourselves."

Ewan pounced on the nearest sack, upending it carelessly. Food and drink rolled across the dirty floor. There were bottles: thick walled and crudely blown. He couldn't remember the last time he'd seen a glass bottle.

He snatched one up and snapped the neck off against the table's edge. Careless of broken glass, Ewan took a deep swallow. It was glorious! Quality wine, sweet and strong. The bouquet filled his head.

"My deepest congratulations," he gasped, once he'd stopped swigging. "I've never tasted anything like this. Where did you find it?"

"It's been a good season in Erberow's vineyards, I believe. Here, I think you may find this more convenient." She offered Ewan a horn cup.

Ewan's hand paused just inches from it. "Erberow? I am unfamiliar with the name." He thought he knew the land beyond Caerbanth. All of the villages and hamlets, right up to the nearest cities. Everywhere was sour and tainted, unable to grow more than a few stunted crops and raise half-starved, deformed livestock.

"It is a garden," said Uryell. "Much like I imagine the one outside was once – but vast and fertile."

"Close by?"

"Not exactly." Ewan couldn't be sure she wasn't mocking him.

After a moment he took the cup and splashed wine into it, ignoring how his hand shook. Perhaps she wasn't mad, but a sorceress instead. Ewan wondered which likelihood was the more dangerous.

He sipped, watching the tall figure as she emptied the second sack across the tabletop, arranging for an impromptu feast. The scattered contents of the first sack were also placed on the board, filling it. Once completed, Uryell sat back in her chair and gestured with her metal arm.

"Please, refresh yourselves. I warrant it's been some time since either of you enjoyed a decent meal."

Feruman laughed bitterly. "You'd be right!" He scooped armfuls closer and began to eat with little restraint, not even sitting.

Uryell glanced at Ewan. "And you? Will you not eat?"

"I'm not hungry." Which was only partly true. His stomach growled at the sight of the meat, bread, fruit and strange cheeses before him, but he would only be able to take down two or three mouthfuls before his body rebelled and nausea took him. Best fill his belly with wine to stave off the pangs. "Perhaps later."

The large catlike creature slinked closer to the table and helped itself to what might have been a fine chicken. Uryell smiled indulgently; again the strange, captivating eyes stayed hard and cold. "If Gra'al has her way, I doubt there will be a later."

Ewan shrugged and picked up a round loaf. It was warm, as though just taken from the oven. Impossible – or so he would have thought earlier. He nibbled at the fresh bread, washing it down with wine, allowing the drink to numb his anxieties.

E WAN SAT AT the high table, sipping a golden wine. The boards before him groaned with the weight of food laid out. Feruman was to his left, bedecked in his finest silks and velvets, laughing secretively with a boy perched on his knee. He was feeding Feruman dark grapes, slipping them between his thin lips, giggling as the Thane tried to suck on his fingers. Feruman looked quite dashing, younger. Ewan had forgotten how handsome he had once been.

The hall was alive with the roar of celebration. The trill of flutes and deeper beat of drums barely ascended above the din. Above it all, hanging from the smoky rafters were six colourful banners: the flags of local guilds, one each in gold, black, silver, blue, white and red. Ewan knew he should recognise them, but the baroque coats of arms flickered and writhed like snake nests, even though the banners themselves were still.

In the open space between the boards and feasting revellers, an ugly, oddly-shaped jester was trying to fight two men dressed as some kind of many-legged dragon. The jester was losing, pounding a twisted, bright golden slapstick against the dragon's scaly costume even as it swallowed him. Ewan laughed at the spectacle – although there was nothing amusing about it.

He tore off a chunk of crusty bread and dipped it into a bowl of sauce. He slipped the morsel into his mouth, disappointed at the bland flavour. He poured more wine into his silver-chased goblet and drank. It too had little to savour.

He turned, looking for a servant to demand better wine – some that wasn't heading towards vinegar – but spotted no one. A portal on his right stood open, as though retainers laden with more choice delights were about to step through at any moment. Yet something about that doorway made Ewan uneasy. He began to wish no one would come through after all.

He looked for Feruman, but the Thane was no longer at his seat. Slunk off with the boy, no doubt.

The sounds of celebration were dimming. The fake dragon, complete with jester dinner, had scuttled away on its multiple legs. The boards were empty. The roaring host had departed to their beds – for sleep or further amusement. Ewan was alone. It occurred to him that he should leave too, while he could.

As Ewan stood, a shadow fell across the open portal. He tried not to see it, but the doorway was filled with a black shape. Ewan's unease blossomed into terror. He backed away, but the boards enclosed him, blocking his exit.

The black shadow stepped closer. It raised an artificial hand—

Ewan snapped awake, gasping. He was sweating, even though the flags under him were icy. Propping himself with unsteady hands he glanced about the empty hall, for a moment wondering where the revellers had gone.

Uryell was sitting cross-legged by the fireplace and its sullen flames, good hand and claws resting in her lap, eyes open but unfocused. Feruman slumped in another corner, snoring impressively. Ewan hoped the man's dreams were less fraught than his own.

The cat creature, Gra'al, padded into the hall, trailing cold air and a faint mist behind it. Its unsettlingly human face was smeared in a thick green ichor, shreds of something pale and diaphanous clung to its claws. It settled at Uryell's feet and began to wash itself, never taking its eyes off Ewan. Eventually, its toilet complete, it dozed.

Ewan stood and reached for a wine bottle standing on the crumb-strewn table. He tipped the bottle against his dry lips. Only a drop fell out. He looked around for another and spotted an unopened one wedged against the bare wall. Somehow it had rolled off the table and survived the fall. Twisting out the stopper he drank, greedily. He wasn't thirsty, and was beginning to loathe the taste of the wine, excellent though it was, but he needed to wash away the sourness in his mouth. And to be drunk. He was desperate for even a touch of oblivion. Yet all but a slight fuzziness evaded him.

Outside, darkness was falling: the blue haze of daylight struggling through the filthy windows slowly dimmed. Ewan had slept the day through. He made his way towards the fireplace and kicked at the dying fire. Sparks flew, but no flames were rekindled. The fuel was practically exhausted. It would burn down soon, making the hall grow ever colder.

He took another drink, wondering what he had agreed to. Everyone knew Cahercrioch was stuffed with fabulous treasure, although he knew of no one who had acted on that certain knowledge. The place was most likely haunted. Ewan refused to speculate on what remained inside the citadel.

Besides, the place scared him. Its history was too ingrained in Gjoranese life for it not to. Even if Cahercrioch wasn't haunted, it certainly haunted Caerbanth.

He took a last drink. As he tilted his head his eyes were caught by the skeleton clock on the opposite wall. For a moment he could have sworn its long-dead mechanism was working again.

There was a harsh snore from Feruman, distracting him. Ewan stared at his lord, silently damning him. He knew greed would banish all of Feruman's doubts, and hated the man for it. Just as he hated himself for his habitual loyalty. His love for Feruman was equal to the disdain which had flourished in their last years together. It would surely get him killed.

"I think it's time."

Ewan started at the deep, liquid voice. Uryell was standing, stretching, reaching for the once ornate ceiling. On the floor, Gra'al was echoing her actions.

Feruman snorted, opening bleary eyes and gazing around in confusion. "Eh?"

Uryell relaxed, her cold green gaze flickering between Ewan and Feruman. "Here. For you." She tapped at a neat bundle on the floor with a toe. Ewan had not spotted it before.

It contained a selection of finely-wrought plate armour along with two sheathed swords. Ewan drew one. Its polished narrow blade glowed a delicate, pale blue. Feruman bared the second – it gleamed a startling white. Ewan had never seen steel tempered to such vibrant colours. Finely-wrought basket hilts curled about the cross guards, so intricate it was hard for the eye to follow. Ewan lifted the pale blue sword high. The balance was perfect, it seemed to weigh nothing. He could have sworn a high keening vibration – almost like a singing voice – came from the blade.

"She likes you," commented Uryell, pale face expressionless. Ewan lowered the weapon, abruptly self-conscious. "I do not joke,

Swordmaster. A good blade will always recognise its master. She is Ezuras. Her sister—" she indicated the pure white sword clutched in Feruman's hand "—is Gwincellor. Treat them well, and fairly, and you will prevail."

Ewan slid the sword back into its sheath with a mumbled word of thanks. He was no Swordmaster. Not for years. He did not deserve such a weapon, but he was loath to surrender it.

Sorting through the pieces of plate, Ewan noticed there was enough to create two sets of half-armour: back and breast plates, arm defences and gauntlets, and tassets to cover the upper part of the legs. There were also two crested burgonet helmets. One set was a dazzling white, the other a pale blue. Ewan did not believe that was a coincidence.

With an ease born of practise – however rusty – he buckled the blue armour on. It was remarkably light and flexible. As a final touch, he belted his sword – Ezuras, was it called? – and scabbard around his waist. With his burgonet nestled in an elbow, he faced Uryell.

"And I suppose such fine suits also came from a place I have never heard of."

She stared back, features unreadable. "Perhaps. Is it important?"

He shook his head, and the tall woman turned her back on him. She fussed a moment over Feruman, who was donning his own white armour with difficulty. Ewan's left hand stroked Ezuras' ornate hilt, momentarily wondering how easy it would be to slip the blue blade into that back, once Cahercrioch's treasures had been safely looted.

Leaving the hall, Ewan cast a final glance at the clock. It was definitely ticking.

They moved quietly through the dead garden, the cat-thing Gra'al close behind them. Beyond the gates, night had fallen. Skeins of gritty fog hugged the uneven ground. The twin moons stared down like unmatched eyes, observing their folly.

Ewan shivered. It was the cold, he told himself. He raised the wine bottle he had brought along, taking two carefully measured sips. For once he would ration himself. Or at least, until they stood outside Cahercrioch.

Above the mansion the slope grew steeper. Within moments Ewan was struggling for breath, his only consolation the sight of Feruman labouring beside him. The other man had donned his burgonet, and where his face showed the flesh was just as white. The only spots of colour were two livid patches on his cheeks, burning feverishly in the moonlight.

As they ascended, Ewan tried to keep his eyes on the ground. It was treacherous, he told himself. In the moon-shot darkness he might miss a step and fall, twist an ankle or knee. Worse, he could smash the bottle before he'd emptied it. It wasn't that he'd rather not look up at the looming Cahercrioch.

Down in Caerbanth the citadel was a distant terror; up close, he could not be sure the sight would unman him.

The ground grew smooth, almost polished. Ewan was aware Uryell had stopped climbing. He halted too, raising his head reluctantly. Before them spread Cahercrioch: a pale brooding mass growing from the slope as though it had once been a living thing. There was no logic to its design. Its wall jutted and flowed, in some parts flat, in others bulging like sores that were about to erupt. Buttresses ran outward for no obvious reason, many ridged like the underside of a mushroom. Towers that looked part animal, part vegetable, grew out of the walls in sagging disarray. Overall rose a crystalline dome, its multiple facets harsh in the moons' light. And before Ewan was some kind of entrance: a pouting, vertical slot in the wall. He shuddered, imagining it a mouth about to open, a huge, thick tongue caressing its lipless edges.

Ewan took a wild, no longer rationed gulp of wine. His free hand settled on the sword at his hip – and something like calm overcame him. He took a deep, even breath. Carefully he stood the almost drained bottle on the ground and drew Ezuras. Distantly he was aware of Feruman at his side, mirroring the action with his own white blade, Gwincellor.

"And now?" Ewan was surprised by how calm he sounded.

Uryell stepped closer to the pouting slit. She reached forward with her silvery left arm. Its claws extended, pinching the lipless mouth, cutting into it. Uryell said something Ewan couldn't quite hear, but he didn't think she spoke any words he knew. The opening puckered, swelled. The slit tried to widen, but was pinned shut by the claws. Uryell wrenched. A huge section of the wall tore free with a loud sucking noise. There was a howl, a wail—

—And something leapt through the gap. Something huge and warty with too many wriggling limbs, and mouths lined with too many teeth. Ewan and Feruman fell back, caught by surprise. The thing advanced, whipping the air.

Uryell stepped in its path. She drew the sword from across her back. It flickered, and a flailing limb spun free. Another slash, and a second coiling arm writhed on the ground. Uryell danced around the thing, striking with a grace and ease that was beyond anything Ewan had ever witnessed. Within moments the creature was down, dissected, leaking a pale violet ichor from its many wounds. The stuff steamed in the cold air.

Uryell cleared her sword blade with a flick of the wrist. Gra'al slunk around her, rubbing affectionately against her legs. Even though he was numb with shock, a part of Ewan's mind still noted Uryell's sword blade did not gleam in the wan moonlight like Ezuras and Gwincellor. Instead, its metal was dull and lifeless, as though it absorbed every ray of moonlight which fell upon it – just as Uryell's dark figure had sucked all of the heat from the fire last night.

She gave the rattled Ewan and Feruman a cursory glance, sparing them no smile this time. Ewan discarded his earlier thoughts of killing her when this was all over. Likely he'd be the one who died.

"Just the first of many such guardians. You must be on your guard. Come, gentlemen." Turning, she entered Cahercrioch. Ewan and Feruman fell in behind, Gra'al at their back.

The gap in the wall did not lead to a keep as Ewan had expected. They stepped instead into a dim, tubular corridor. In the shadows it appeared endless. Uryell was running her metal arm along a curved wall as though searching for something. As Ewan wondered if she was about to once again rip the wall apart, the woman exclaimed softly. A soft glow filled the space, the light coming from a bright, shifting spiral which ran the length of the corridor, twisting and rotating slowly as though alive.

Without a word, Uryell moved forward, her sword at the ready.

The two men followed just as silently, although Ewan thought he could hear a voice – barely a whisper – at the limit of his hearing. He glanced at Feruman, but the Thane's lips were tightly closed. Was it the strange twisting light, or did Feruman look younger? His sharpened features softer? More as he had in Ewan's dream. He certainly walked straighter, his recent, habitual crouch gone. He looked calm, confident. He held Gwincellor as though born with the sword in his hand.

Ewan wondered if he too looked as poised. He felt more self-assured – more than he had been in years. More than he had a right to. He glanced sidelong at the blue sword he carried, straining to hear the distant voice. A suspicion grew in his mind.

The coiling light source abruptly went out. Ewan heard a scuffle, a grunt, the hum of steel. He raised his sword, trying to pierce the sudden darkness with old eyes that took too long to adjust. There was a soft cry, a sob – and the light returned.

Ewan blinked. The corridor had gone. Now they stood in a high vaulted chamber, the ceiling lost in shadow. The arching walls were etched with a network of fine traceries that gently pulsed with blue and red light. Occasionally the light would flicker and dim, and when it returned not all of the network was restored. Ewan saw patches where the traceries were black and dead, the wall ready to crumble. So this place was decaying as much as Caerbanth. For some reason it was an unsettling thought.

Uryell was standing over an oozing corpse, sword in hand. Whatever she had killed seemed to have bat-like wings. It was rapidly liquefying. Gra'al crouched nearby, watching it carefully, a low buzzing in its throat. Against one flickering wall slumped Feruman, his lifeblood pumping through a rent in his burgonet and down his breastplate. Where it had sprayed over the wall it mimicked the traceries of light.

Ewan let out a low moan.

"Gwincellor could not save him." Uryell stooped and pulled the white sword from slack fingers, unbuckling the sword belt. She straightened, glanced in Ewan's direction and frowned. "I am ... sorry."

To Ewan it sounded as though Uryell was simply repeating a phrase she had been taught, with no real understanding. "Thank you," he said, anyway.

Uryell and Gra'al stepped away from the two bodies. The woman seemed to be searching for something. She had sheathed Gwincellor and now wore it on her right hip.

"What about Feruman?" Ewan felt it wrong to simply abandon him. He had been his Thane once, after all. And his friend.

"What of him? He is dead now, and Cahercrioch's treasures lie ahead. Or had you forgotten?"

Uryell's mockery stung him. Did she consider him so shallow? A tired old drunk who only cared where his next drink came from...?

He sighed. Of course she did. What else was there for her to behold?

Ewan followed the woman and cat-thing across the vast chamber. Their footsteps made no sound, as though they trod the thickest of carpets rather than what looked like polished stone. Uryell found another corridor, narrow and low-ceilinged, lit by rows of yellow cubes which gave off a brilliant white light, but no heat. Murals covered the walls: scenes so abstract, their patterns so complex, they befuddled Ewan's brain. He could make little sense of them.

"Where are we going?" It occurred to Ewan that Uryell was leading with far too much confidence.

"To the *velanke'en*."

Whatever that meant. "You seem to know Cahercrioch well."

"The Chulainn were a predictable race. Their designs equally so."

"Were?"

Uryell glanced back. This time her smile was as cold as her eyes. "We have arrived."

They stepped into another chamber. Not as vast as the first, this was irregularly shaped, with walls that tottered at dangerous angles. There was not a straight line to be seen. Light from hidden sources splashed across the warped surfaces in random, shifting patterns that fooled the eye even more. Throughout the chamber were great sheets of glass or polished crystal, hanging on invisible supports, or growing from the uneven floor. The only flat things visible. Across every smooth surface danced images, the entire chamber was a chaos of disconnected, moving pictures. Scenes of Caerbanth, the blighted land beyond, the mountains – all these Ewan recognised, even though they blazed with false, disturbing colours and were often out of proportion. Other scenes were unfamiliar, the stuff of dreams.

Endless plains of black and gold, across which rolled countless transparent pebbles, as though alive; blue and yellow forests choked with crystalline trees, and leathery sheets which flapped purposefully above the canopy; churning oceans of green water in which swam things Ewan couldn't begin to describe; black skies misted by numberless points of light against which floated rocky globes.

Was this what lay beyond Gjoran? Or further still? Uryell had mentioned other worlds...

"You promised treasure!" Ewan's mind seized on a familiar concept in the face of insanity.

Uryell gestured at the chamber's unsettling angles, the bizarre images. "It lies before you. All the wealth Cahercrioch could ever need. Her heart, the source of her power. Once the womb of her life: a *velanke'en*."

Ewan shook his head in denial. Tricked—!

Four figures stood before him. They entered through no door, but were simply there. Tall and thin like Uryell, also clothed in black, and bearing similar long swords. But where Uryell's features were fine and delicate, their faces were coarse, their hair corpse-grey, and their eyes the colour of old blood.

Uryell and Gra'al leapt forward. She moved across the uneven floor like a dancer. Each thrust, parry, block, duck and leap part of an intricate web of motion. Her huge pet was a lithe, unstoppable knot of muscle. In contrast, Ewan fought clumsily against a pallid creature which itself moved like a stabbing blade. Every one of Ewan's thrusts impaled empty air, every parry nothing more than a blind, panicked response. His opponent was in all places, yet none of them.

Certain of death, Ewan staggered back as he clumsily blocked another blow. The unaccustomed armour overbalanced him and he slipped, landing heavily, the breath driven from his lungs. Helpless, he gazed up at the sword raised for the death stroke.

His sword hand moved of its own volition. The pale blue sword blocked the descending blade, shattering it. Ezuras seemed to be alive, taking control of Ewan's right arm. Its blade was a blur as it responded faster than his eye could follow. The grey creature stumbled, almost falling, clutching its throat. Another flicker of blue, and the living corpse's own sword spun across the chamber, bouncing off a tall flat sheet depicting winged snakes chasing down tiny humans. A strike, and the thing died without a sound.

In a daze, Ewan came to his feet. The other three corpse-faced things were down, melting away just as the bat-winged creature had. Gra'al lay across one body, its paws and muzzle strangely unbloodied.

There was a look on Uryell's pale face which scared Ewan more than the thing which had almost killed him. "Would that they had been real," she sighed. In the uncertain light it looked as though her pupils had vertical slits, like a cat's.

"Not real? One almost killed me!"

"Not living as you understand it. Ectypes. Subtle replicas."

Ewan turned away, his mind whirling. The dismaying images all around him were more intoxicating than any amount of wine. Power, Uryell had said. The sort of power which guarded a long-abandoned citadel with solid creatures; which looked out across the world like a sentinel on a tower. He took a step towards one hanging sheet of crystal, both drawn and repulsed by its awful fascination.

The sudden pain was cold and remote. He looked down to see the angled tip of a curved, silvery blade jutting from his breastplate. Ripples spread across the pale blue metal from where it contacted the sword blade.

"None of this is for you, little Ewan." Uryell's deep voice whispered intimately in his ear.

Ewan could feel the blade running through his body, scraping against backbone, puncturing lung and heart, exiting past his breastbone. Why was he not dead?

"You are dead." Uryell murmured as though she could hear Ewan's chaotic thoughts. "A little of the *mandra'al* power in my left arm also flows through you, keeping your mind aware."

Ewan tried to speak through rapidly numbing lips. "W-what are you—?"

"I am Uryell. An Inquisitor. What you observe in this chamber are windows upon the Internection – a mere handful of its infinite Tiers. The nearest, where this *velanke'en* had most influence. There are rules which govern those Tiers, and we enforce them in whichever way we find necessary. I was too late here, your world is almost drained, but it's not too late to save this Tier. The *velanke'en* will be replete, gorged on nearby stars and planets. It will be slow, careless. I can easily track it, wherever it has fled. And I can certainly destroy its old nest."

The blade withdrew and Ewan collapsed to the floor. Through blurred eyes he saw a long, slightly curved blade retreat into the steel arm, below the claws. The unreadable markings glowed softly. Uryell looked down at him. Her smile was regretful.

"You are a drunk, likely a thief, but I don't think you are, at heart, a bad man, Das Ewan. So I regret I have not been entirely honest with you. With the *velanke'en* gone, this citadel is dying – taking your world with it. But if a soul is fused in its place, there may still be time to reverse the entropy. Would you give your life to resurrect what remains of Gjoran and the lands beyond? You will not be hailed as this world's saviour – for who will know? – but it will be the truth, nonetheless."

Ewan tried to speak, to ask if he could just have a drink instead. His body refused to respond.

Uryell raised the fluid metal arm and spoke a word. Its echo resounded throughout the chamber: reverberations which never quite ended. As Ewan's sight fled with his life he heard an agonised scream.

❦❦❦

THE RESIDUAL TRACES of the *velanke'en* drained from the screen-walls. Uryell stepped back as the decay splashed against their black clothing, warming it. A moment later every screen shattered. Needle shards covered the uneven floor, then even they melted and boiled away.

"About time."

Uryell spun about, sword raised. A greybeard in a long dark robe stood not two arm's lengths away, leaning on a tall black staff. Despite the ancient flowing locks and beard his black eyes twinkled with mischief, his voice that of someone a fraction of his apparent age. Gra'al sprawled on the floor and ignored the newcomer, preferring to lick her paws.

Uryell lowered their sword point. "Raven! How did you come here?"

The other grinned. "Good to see you too. You're not hard to find – all those bodies in your wake. And once you disabled the screen-walls, the way was open." He glanced at the black feline. "Hello, Gra'al."

The cat-creature's ears flicked, but she paid the newcomer no more attention.

He sniffed. "Still not forgiven me, then."

Uryell returned the longsword to its sheath, green eyes fixed on the black staff. It looked innocuous, but even if the runes along their metal arm weren't blazing with recognition, they would have known it. A *mandra'al* staff, a spindle about which the base matter of the Internection might be woven. One of only three ever forged.

"Where did you get it?"

Raven glanced at the staff as though he was only just aware of its presence. "This? Oh, you gave it to me – or will give it to me." His impish grin widened. "You know how it goes. Here."

Carelessly he tossed the staff towards Uryell. Of its own volition their metal arm reached out and nimbly caught the black shaft in their claws. The runes flared brighter still. A pale blue glow outlined the staff. "Will I be needing it?"

The greybeard shrugged. "One of us will, and I imagine we will be better served with it in your hands. As it were."

"Why?"

Raven's face grew serious. "The Internection has been breached. Something which has no business outside its own sealed corner of the Boundless has entered. I still don't know how, or why, but it must be found and removed."

"Does this something have a name?"

"Fatecaster."

Uryell grunted. The term was familiar: from stories told among

Eternals when even they were young. "You are certain?"

"As certain as I can be." Raven was grinning again. "Besides, I met him once – or will do." He tapped his high forehead. "It's all up here. I just need to work out the sequence." He nodded towards the staff. "Just follow its lead, my friend. It's closer to the Source than anything since the Progenitor."

"And you?"

"I have clues to unravel. Places to visit, people to see. You know me."

"Only too well."

Raven laughed. "But before I go—" he indicated the sword on Uryell's hip, and the other lying close to Ewan's body "—I'll be needing those." He tutted and shook his head. "Ezuras and Gwincellor? Two Swords of Fate together? And they call me reckless."

Uryell took up Ezuras and Gwincellor, handing them over to the greybeard. "I needed at least one to reach the screen-wall chamber. Neither would have survived beyond the first gate without them."

Raven pursed his lips. "You're far too hard-headed for my taste, Inquisitor Uryell." He shrugged. "Ah well – farewell for now. We shall meet again – somewhen." He bowed, raising both arms in a complex gesture. A moment later he was gone. Gra'al raised her massive head and glanced about, grey eyes curious.

Uryell looked at the tall staff, contemplating their next action. As though prompted by their thoughts, the blue glow about the staff intensified, filling the chamber with a frigid light.

There was an explosion of impossible magnitude. The veils between the Tiers of the Internection were briefly torn aside.

Cahercrioch was erased from existence, settling like dust across Caerbanth and the lands beyond.

THE RAINS OF BAROFONN

TWO FIGURES PERCHED on top of a high, barren cliff. They hid behind a grey, cleft rock, gazing down on a ruined plain which spread, unbroken, from the foot of the cliff as far as the misted horizon. They were reptilian creatures, their eyes raised high on scaly green heads, long jaws coming to a beaked point. They were dressed in ornate crested helmets and lacquered plate armour which fitted them badly, clearly designed for anatomies far different from their own. Long curved swords hung at their sides. Their black eyes reflected the simplest of intellects.

A bitter wind blew across the cliff top, finding its way through every gap in the ill-fitting armour, slowly cooling the figures to a dangerous level. They would not be able to stay for much longer, their reptilian bodies would chill to the point of rigid torpor. The thin, mauve sun hanging low in the sky radiated little heat.

Both were watching a distant figure cross the plain, carrying a tall staff. They nodded at each other and grunted. This must be the one they were meant to report on.

Scrambling away from the cliff face, down a steep scree slope, they made for two spindly creatures which seemed to be part fish, part giant mantis. Hauling themselves awkwardly into crude saddles, the armoured figures goaded their spindle-legged mounts away from the plain and down towards Grafanox.

The outer walls of the city, sitting at the foot of the Black Mountains, encompassed a sprawling collection of ugly grey buildings, none higher than two floors. All looked tired and stooping with age. Once inside the walls, the armoured riders forced their strange mounts through dense, reluctant crowds. The city's reptilian population treated the riders with practised indifference, reacting only to the lash of a barbed foreleg or flared mandibles. The pair were clearly making for the ornate citadel carved into the mountain face which overlooked the city. Long ago Grafanox's lord, the Tréarq, had entered that black and silver structure and never re-emerged. As the slow-witted inhabitants considered it, acknowledging either the structure, or any of those who came and went through its gates, might invite a similar fate.

The riders were let into the citadel's central keep by guards clad in similar armour, although their features and shapes were even more alien and varied. The mounts were led away by blue skinned things which had neither head nor arms, just thickly furred prehensile wings and clawed feet, their eyes buried deep within the folds of those wings. Passing through wide double doors, the armoured reptiles made their way along a brightly-lit, high vaulted corridor. Its walls were lined with designs and frescos which may have been strange works of art, or forms of machinery beyond their understanding. They averted their eyes, no more eager to look at the flickering patterns than those outside had wished to acknowledge them. There was a distant, rhythmic pulse: a heartbeat, the throb of a drum, deep breathing.

A door swung wide at their approach, although there was none to move it. They stepped into a vast chamber where silvered walls flickered with light of every hue. At the far end, on a high throne shaped like a delicate pink crystal shot through with gold veins, sat a creature which changed its shape with every beat of the distant throb. As though its body was composed of countless restless worms it fleshed out, thinned, grew tall, short. Its eyes ranged from slits to vast orbs, from stalks to polyps. Limbs grew and lost bone, both outside and internally. They became fleshy tendrils, briefly grew thick chitin, sprouted suckers, claws, or delicate fingers. The head was a red welt, a vast nodding canker, a gaudy blossom, its features rearranging themselves into recognisable organs, or growths which had no discernible purpose. Although there was never more than one head, the number of limbs changed constantly. It motioned the riders to approach with a green frond which instantly transformed into a fat pseudopod.

They each dropped to one knee, removing their ornate helmets and bowing their heads.

"Well?" The voice, issuing from no obvious source, was low and seductive.

"Master," croaked one. "We seed un. Out in desert. Coming to Grafanox."

The face split wide, pale stamens wriggled in the fissure, each bearing a yellow eye. "You are certain it was the one?"

They both nodded. "Certain, master."

"Did they have a companion?"

"No, master. Un was alone."

Waving a pallid flipper, shape ebbing and flowing, their master sank back against the crystal throne. "Very well, you may go."

They bowed and retreated, thankful the interview had been so short.

❦ ❈ ❦

THE RESTIVE SHAPE on the throne watched his two reptilian guards shamble away. They were poor material for a scouting party – far too slow and literal – but he had little else to work with. At least they had carried out their orders with as great a degree of efficiency as they could.

He half-turned, the movement conducted more by his flowing body altering its shape.

"Prosskaa!"

A door, hidden behind the throne, swung open. A tall creature with colourless, staring eyes and an expressionless, yellow-scaled head stepped through. A ruff of sharp spines and fins around its face may have been part of its baroque armour. Turning to face the throne, it bowed low.

"You heard?"

Prosskaa inclined its spiny head.

"Bring the Inquisitor to us. Quickly."

Prosskaa bowed again. "As you command, Lord Shilnoth." It retreated, head still lowered, to the concealed door which closed silently behind it, once more undetectable.

Shilnoth the Shapeless, sometimes called the Many Shaped, settled back on the throne. As predicted, green-eyed Uryell had arrived. Now to secure them.

CONCEALED IN A niche above the main gates, Uryell watched the townsfolk of Grafanox queuing for their daily ration of water and food. Covered in dull black clothing, the Inquisitor would be all but impossible to spot against the shadows – only the delicate, pallid face and pale red hair stood out to any degree. Their cold green eyes were hooded. The flowing metal left arm had become dull and muted, the runes which covered it presently grey and lifeless.

Although not normally given to idle speculation, Uryell could not help but wonder why, of all the realms of the Boundless, the infinite Tiers of the Internection, the *mandra'al* staff had chosen desolate Barofonn. The Inquisitor remembered the world when it had been ripe and fertile.

And no Gra'al this time. Uryell's quasi-feline companion had not transitioned, for reasons known only to the Source. And there would be a reason, of that there could be no doubt. Nonetheless, she would be missed.

Uryell rested a narrow, pointed ear against the black staff so recently provided by meddlesome Raven. For his own reasons, no doubt. The three *mandra'al* staffs were thought by some to actually be remnants of the Progenitor. They certainly commanded the warp and weft of the Boundless, able to wrap the Internection's endless Tiers about themselves. Perhaps they were even sentient. Uryell could almost sense a remote, cold intelligence deep within the staff, removed from the physical object by many dimensional twists. The Inquisitor even fancied it communicated, on some level, although they did not need the staff to tell them there was a *velanke'en* lurking within the citadel.

Uryell was grateful the *mandra'al* staff had brought them hither: the destruction of any *velanke'en* was of prime importance. But the Inquisitor felt it was not the only reason they had been drawn.

If the staff knew, it did not share the information. Or at least, not on any conscious level.

An armoured party emerged from the citadel gate, impatiently pushing the queuing reptiles aside. It was composed of races not native to Barofonn: yellow-scaled Ixssaashi, crimson dog-faced Cyrofache, even a handful of grey-haired Chulainn. They climbed into saddles strapped to tall, many-legged fish-insect things of a species unfamiliar to the Inquisitor, and made towards the approaching twilight.

Uryell patiently waited for the food queue to dissipate and

darkness to fall. Gradually Grafanox became silent, except for a soft, acrid wind blowing in from the desert. Holding the black staff carefully, Uryell slipped from the niche, landing silently on the dusty ground.

The high gate was shut and barred. Uryell touched the staff against the ancient, half-fossilised wood and pressed an ear against the rough surface. There was a single guard beyond. Complacency, or bluff? Uryell's full lips twitched: either they took the Inquisitor for a fool, or wished to create that impression.

Caution was advised.

There was a narrow gap where the old timbers had shrunk, not much wider than a fist. Uryell transferred the staff to the pincers protruding from their rune-marked left arm of flowing silvery metal. Easing the staff through the gap, the metal arm shifting subtly as the slumbering runes partly awoke, allowing Uryell to slip it through the gap, they rotated the staff until it was horizontal, then pulled it flat against the back of the gate. Anchoring it firmly. Drawing in a deep breath, the Inquisitor urged the staff's command over Space and Time to also awake. *Mandra'al* energy glowed along the staff's length: pale blue light just visible through gaps in the shrunken timbers. It also spread gradually up the metal arm; gently, so as not to awake any alarms within the citadel or alert the so far unmindful guard. The runes took on a brighter glow of their own.

Uryell pulled against the anchoring staff, their tall frame flowing into the narrow gap, twisting, stretching. Spun upon a *mandra'al* loom, forcibly transitioned down sub-Tiers in order to wrench matter through a physical space that was otherwise far too narrow. Body warped almost flat, Uryell endured an agony that was beyond physical pain.

For a moment they were blind to everything beyond that torment.

Then the gate was at their back. Beyond was the keep. The excruciating pain became a distant, fading ache.

The single Cyrofache guard turned. Before it could call out, Uryell drew the longsword sheathed across their back and beheaded the dog-faced creature with an efficient slash.

Keeping low, the Inquisitor ran silently across the keep, heading towards a building that by its very ostentation proclaimed its importance. Halting at towering double doors which were carved into gaudy patterns, Uryell scanned the keep one last time before slipping inside. Through a door opened no more than necessary.

Two Ixssaashi stood at ease within a frescoed corridor. Uryell waited as they turned their backs to plod down the corridor, before slipping into their tracks, sword raised. Two lightning-swift strikes and both yellow-scaled creatures were dead without a sound. Cold green blood from their severed necks pooled on the tiled floor.

There was a narrow, unlit passage leading off the larger corridor. Uryell paused, eyes flicking between the *mandra'al* staff and passageway. The staff was uncommunicative, generating no sense of either danger or safety. That in itself could be more than a warning. The Inquisitor returned their longsword to its back sheath and slipped into the darkness, right hand brushing along the wall. Feeling, listening.

The passageway turned sharply to the left, rising. A moment later it plunged in a steep, smooth drop. With each of Uryell's steps the corridor shifted direction: rising, falling, doubling back on itself. It was a spiral, a cone. It constricted so that the Inquisitor had to crawl, it expanded so abruptly the fingertips brushing the wall briefly lost contact. Peristaltic waves quivered under Uryell's touch.

The Inquisitor stood in a vast chamber, the ceiling so high it was lost in murky shadow. To either side the walls were lined by towering figures. Statues, Uryell thought, carved from a bright, glistening stone that refracted every hue. The colours shimmered, giving an impression of movement. They were obese, avian shapes, covered in what – at first glance – looked like huge feathers. A closer inspection revealed they were fractal differentials of the figures themselves, imitating each colossus in decreasing scale. Each statue was composed from countless versions of itself.

Uryell smiled. It was a conceit with which they were familiar. A clue as to why the staff had brought them to this otherwise desolate place? Certainly one as to who else occupied the citadel, along with the *velanke'en*. Curious companions, though.

As Uryell stepped cautiously between the rows, the bulbous, beaked heads turned fractionally, always keeping deceptively blank eyes on the Inquisitor. So, not just an impression of movement after all. Nor lifeless statues, either.

The chamber narrowed, opening into a shapeless compartment filled with interlaced, rainbow light. Perched on a huge white crystal sat a creature both more and less human than the Inquisitor. Gangling, spidery limbs wove around its tiny body. Its oversized head gazed at the opalescent light pulsing along a complex web which grew from the crystal and crowded the void. Pyramidal structures glowed with a pale violet, sprouting like fungus from the floor and ceiling. Despite the overall radiance, the features of the creature perched upon the crystal were in constant shadow.

The rainbow flashed brighter, reaching a crescendo. Uryell squinted. The lights dimmed abruptly, the glistening web becoming no more than a softly glowing mass of threads. The Inquisitor stepped closer to the room's strange occupant, grounding the black staff. Its black material seemed to hum, the vibration radiating up along Uryell's metal arm. A sense of recognition.

"Welcome," chirped the spindly creature. "This is an untimely meeting."

Uryell bowed low, beginning the ritual. "*Velanke'en*. I bring the finality of the Source."

The *velanke'en* winced at the other's words. It shifted uncomfortably but seemed unable to move from its perch.

"Before Creation, the Progenitor sat in the very centre of the Void; in her right hand a pearl, a diamond in her left." From their black clothing Uryell pulled a fragment which glowed with a dull, white light. It was thin, shapeless: a scrap of torn cloth or paper. "First she contemplated the pearl: its pure white lustre and perfect symmetry of surface. Then her gaze wandered to the diamond, and was instantly captured. She looked at the billion, billion facets, the limitless internal refractions, and saw that each held a reflection of her face. Yet not a single image was like another, and none was a true reflection. As she gazed, she became confident that it was the infinite number of faces which were real, and she a composite reflection of a Boundless Reality. So, with a laugh, she crushed the diamond, releasing Creation."

The *velanke'en* raised its face out of shadow. Colourless eyes sparkled like myriad-faceted stones, set in unformed, pasty embryonic features. "Yet was the Progenitor not destroyed?" it responded.

"The expanding Internection tore her essence apart; thus she became the Source."

"Did she choose wrongly?"

"No. And so it was she laughed." Uryell raised the fragment on an outstretched right hand and blew. It fluttered, drifting up towards the *velanke'en*.

The chamber erupted into life. Dimensional space ceased to have meaning. Inquisitor and *velanke'en* were colossi filling the universe. They were motes of existence smaller than an atom. Nameless colours coruscated around them.

The fragment struck the *velanke'en*, and darkness fell. The spindly, nascent creature blinked into non-existence. All that remained was a dazzling speck, hanging motionless.

The fragment, no longer dull, burned with an opalescence which etched the Inquisitor's features. They squinted against the awful light. It descended gradually, enclosing Uryell with a swirling, silver-white lustre. The Inquisitor waited, listening to the chamber's death-throes. It moaned and creaked as the power centre crumbled.

With an almost sentient cry, the web shattered. The ceiling imploded. The chamber was filled with choking grey dust.

The walls fell.

SHILNOTH SAT AT a low table, playing a complex board game with the Tréarq of Barofonn. The old scars and fresh welts on the beaked, reptilian head were a testament to the time he had spent as the Shapeless One's guest. His shrunken, abused body was hidden by loose, richly decorated robes. Two scabbards hung from his girdled waist. As propriety dictated, both were empty.

Shilnoth hesitated, waiting for the limb hovering above one game piece to develop some means by which he might hold it. Segmented fingers sprouted. He was about to take one of the Tréarq's pieces when agonising pain seared through his body. Shilnoth's form erupted with jagged blades and gaping, tooth-filled maws. He dropped his game piece. It shattered on the floor.

The pain subsided. Shilnoth reformed into a mass of soothing waves and gently undulating tendrils. "The *velanke'en!*" His normally seductive voice was broken and raw.

The Tréarq leaned forward with interest. "*Velanke'en*? Source of your power?" Despite Shilnoth's best efforts to keep the dull creature in ignorance, over the years it was inevitable that he would learn something of the citadel's inner workings, no matter how imperfectly.

Shilnoth ignored him. He hissed as another freezing spasm threatened to crack open his fluid innards.

"Is well?" The Tréarq's long nails caressed the locket of one empty scabbard.

Shilnoth swept a limb across the board, scattering the pieces. He made for the throne, staggering with each new assault. His plastic form flailed and lashed. He felt the tremors as the power centre imploded. He heard cries of pain and terror.

The Tréarq's dull eyes watched carefully

Shilnoth collapsed onto the throne, leaning heavily on the arms. His body seethed, threatening to overflow the crystal. The Tréarq came to his feet and hobbled towards Shilnoth, one hand held out as if in sympathy, the other still resting on the scabbard. His eyes showed no emotion.

"I help." The Tréarq's claw on the scabbard released a catch. The locket became a three bladed dagger. He stood over the squirming Shilnoth, weapon poised.

One of Shilnoth's limbs annealed into a long, crude blade. Despite his agony, the Many-Shaped thrust upwards, spearing the Tréarq's throat. As the creature flopped away, black blood staining his ornate robes, Shilnoth caught him in a nest of fanged tentacles. Feeding off the other's pain, the Shapeless One found the strength to rip the Tréarq apart.

Shilnoth reabsorbed the stained blade. He could taste the Tréarq's blood. It was invigorating. "We indulged you far too long."

Another groan rose through the fabric of the citadel: the building voicing its death throes. Shilnoth flowed for the hidden door.

URYELL STEPPED INTO a dusty street. Ahead of them, Shilnoth was limping through the high gate on his ever changing limbs. The Shapeless One halted when he saw the Inquisitor, head splitting wide to reveal a shark's grin.

Uryell pointed the *mandra'al* staff. "Shilnoth, as I had suspected.

He whose schemes multiply with each novel form. What have you done, Many Shapes?"

"Other than brought you to us?" A hairy armoured creature waved several prehensile trunks at Uryell's staff and laughed. "Many things. Among them underestimating both you and the brainless ruler of this dead city." For a moment, Shilnoth was a beautiful youth, his body symmetrical, perfect. For once his form matched his voluptuous voice. He shrugged. "No matter."

"You have lost this *velanke'en*—"

"Do you think it is our only one?" Shilnoth staggered as one leg became a wriggling vine. His head morphed into a needle-beaked bird. "We have been harvesting *velanke'en* from across the Boundless, with the Chulainn only too eager to help." He giggled: a grotesque, coquettish sound coming from deep inside a mass of sharp leaves. "They think we mean to help them subdue the Internection..."

"If only your ambition was so small."

"You understand us so well, dear Uryell."

The Inquisitor rapped the *mandra'al* staff into the dust. The city's walls quivered, brick crumbled. "This staff brought me hither, Many Shapes. It did not do so merely because you seek to defraud the Chulainn. I understand the Internection has been breached."

"Then you understand more than we!" Shilnoth became a crystalline outgrowth, around his head a halo of carnelian lips pouted. "Of course that stick dragged you to Barofonn. Ripples, Inquisitor – all spreading from a single disturbance. Easier that you come to us than we go in search of you. You rigid minded androgynes are so predictable."

Uryell paused. Shilnoth was frequently vainglorious, but never reckless with his own life. Had the Inquisitor been lured? Been overconfident?

A bulbous sac sprouted from Shilnoth's left side. It grew upwards on a waving stalk, towering over them both. As its growth slowed the sac opened, peeling back like a bud. Nestled within was a colourless gemstone the size of the Inquisitor's right hand. It rose into the air, flickering to life.

Uryell raised the *mandra'al* staff, preparing for an attack.

"Do you not recognise it?" The bud and stalk withered, shrinking back into Shilnoth's torso. The Shapeless One spread mismatched limbs. "It is a Nexus Jewel, of course. Plundered from some long-forgotten Node World, then lost here, on Barofonn."

Uryell was unconvinced. "It is too small."

"You are disingenuous, Inquisitor. You know size is relative." Several spider eyes rose to the surface of Shilnoth's head and stared up at the floating jewel. "Uniquely, here in this desolate place, a Nexus Jewel may appear as nothing more than a plain, slightly oversized bauble. The very reason it has been overlooked for so long, perhaps." The eyes flowed together; the entire head became a single eyeball. "And small though it is, this gem houses the combined essences of every mature *velanke'en* we have harvested."

The gem erupted solid light. Caught unawares, Uryell barely had time to deflect the impact with the *mandra'al* staff. The Inquisitor was thrown to the ground, dropping their staff. The power in that single ray was greater than anything Uryell had ever endured.

A hydra of wriggling limbs swept out of Shilnoth, knotting

themselves around the fallen staff. Uryell snatched for it. Fingers and pincers closed on emptiness.

Shilnoth grounded the staff, leaning his unstable form against it. The bright, hovering gemstone dipped, attaching itself to the raised tip. A dark glow ran along the staff's length as the Nexus Jewel dimmed to a blood red.

"Thank you, dearest Inquisitor." Shilnoth smiled down at Uryell from a face composed of interlocking teeth. "Now we have all we need, it is time for us to leave."

An intense beam spat from the gem. Silvery arm raised, the runes along it glowing white hot, Uryell barely managed to repel the shaft of light. It ran to ground through the Inquisitor's body. A river of agony.

"What about Fatecaster?" Uryell could barely speak.

Shilnoth paused. "Tales to frighten mortals or newly-hatched spawn? We're disappointed."

"It crept through ... when the Internection was breached—" The Inquisitor reached within themself for the thin bright mote that was all that remained of Barofonn's *velanke'en*. It shifted, reluctant, scared. "If that breach ... was of your doing—" The mote oozed through Uryell's pale skin, distilling into a tiny glimmer, suspended between the tips of their metal pincers.

"You sound like that interfering Raven. I have done nothing – save what you see. However—" Shilnoth took a step closer, lowering the staff to point its mounted jewel directly at Uryell. Another agonising shaft of light struck the Inquisitor.

Uryell pushed the agony aside, enclosed it within their mind.

Acknowledged its existence while holding themselves apart from it.

They were puzzled. Shilnoth was no dissembler – far too vain for such subtlety – yet the Shapeless One's denial had the ring of truth. He knew nothing of Fatecaster, or the injury to the Boundless...

Because, for Shilnoth, it had yet to happen.

"Raven! You devious—"

The tiny mote held in the Inquisitor's pincers flared. Glowing with its own actinic light, runes ablaze, Uryell's silvery arm snapped out, catapulting the gleaming particle directly into the beam. At first there was no response. Uryell thought their gamble had failed. Then the speck grew brighter, matching the Nexus Jewel. The tiny spot of brilliance expanded, gorging upon the multiple *velanke'en* essences, swollen by them. It became an incandescent ball. A small sun.

It shattered.

A SOUNDLESS BLAZE LIT the night sky. Above, the dead plain black clouds stacked up, growing and multiplying. The air grew thick and humid. When day broke the sky was so choked by clouds that the weary, mauve sun could not break through. Many were convinced the world was ending.

Rain began to fall.

Starting as a light shower, it grew heavier, gaining ferocity until it was a deluge cascading through narrow alleys and broad streets, tearing a pathway through the citadel and outer city until it seemed all of Grafanox would be washed out into the cold desert. For twenty days the downpour continued, stopping as abruptly as it had begun.

The black clouds evaporated, leaving the skies clear and fresh.

When the inhabitants finally dared creep from their homes, they found the silver and black citadel an unrecognisable ruin. Of the strange creatures which had terrorised and abused them, there was no sign.

Just beyond the ancient gates they found an area of gleaming fused sand. Around it, peeking through the wet clay, were tiny seedlings. In the very centre of the black glass, unnoticed and insignificant, was a tiny white fragment. Dull and lifeless. Embedded forever.

65

THE POWER OF THE SERPENT

HE AWOKE WITH a start, breath hitching, heart resounding in his chest. His hand was already halfway to the hilt of the golden sword hung on the wall above his bed, within easy reach. He paused, forcing his breathing to even out, his heart to calm, and listened. There were no cries of alarm, no shrieks of terror. The floor beneath his bed stayed resolutely still. The night was still.

Mournar, Emperor, for over thirty years feared ruler of the Lęnj-Ńowić Empire, lowered the hand seeking the hilt of his great golden sword, Krysolac, and slowly lay back among his bed's disordered sheets. It was a dream, then. Just a dream. Although one so real.

Or was it simply that he so seldom dreamed his mind was unable to separate the fantasy from reality.

Mournar reached for the lamp guttering by his bedside and turned up its wick. The surging flame cast a pool of yellow light across the great bed, its four grotesquely-carved posts, and a little way further into his chamber. Shadows capered across the dim walls, the hangings which covered them – although the lamplight did not penetrate far enough to pick out their unique, bespoke designs – and the great doors which were carved with patterns as bizarre as his bedposts, but they were familiar shadows. He had seen them cast thousands of times since he had seized the imperial crown.

He turned to the shape lying beside him, covered by a sheet. Since he was awake, the girl could provide him with more distraction. The gods knew she had cost enough. He pulled back the sheet, barely noticing the dark stains dried across it. Underneath, large blue eyes stared up at him, her lips parted – just so. Mournar leaned closer, starting to grin, his tongue flicking over his unusually long, sharp canine teeth, then drew back abruptly.

Her eyes continued to stare blankly, the lips slack.

He pulled the sheet away entirely. Her exposed body was cut and peeled, incised expertly and imaginatively. A painting in blood, a flayed sculpture, a lesson in anatomy and suffering. And unfortunately dead.

Mournar roared a curse and flung the sheet back over the corpse. Petye had sworn she was of tough peasant stock, strong and vital, that the Emperor would be able to enjoy her until well past dawn.

He swung himself out of bed, grabbing the lamp with some vague idea of throwing it on the bed and enjoying the sight of the thoughtless bitch engulfed in flames. For a moment his rage was great enough to mask the dull aches and stiffness his body had begun to endure of late, but it did not last. The pain won as his fury abated, an unwelcome reminder that even he was succumbing to age.

He rubbed harshly at his beard, driving away the last vestiges of sleep. That at least was the same deep brown it had ever been, with no indication of grey or silver. The same with his thick, tousled hair. And he knew that outwardly he had changed not at all. It was his bones, sinews and muscle which betrayed him rather than his looks, and he had always been markedly handsome – even with the suggestion of fangs and his long, equally sharp-pointed ears. Even before he had donned the ceremonial dress of state no one had ever failed to recognise Mournar the mercenary. Mournar the general.

He replaced the lamp and snatched up a robe to cover his own naked, bloodied body. Tying the robe about him he flung wide his chamber door and stepped into the grand drawing room beyond. It was lit by many wall-mounted lamps, all turned down, leaving the room, its furnishings, and the numerous artworks adorning the panelled walls bathed in the faintest of warm, roseate glows.

"Petye!" The procured girl might be beyond his pleasures, but by all the gods if he couldn't enjoy her flesh he would indulge himself in his First Minister's. "Petye!"

There was no answering call, no pounding of agitated feet propelling the minister to his master's side, eager to placate him in any way possible. Mournar grinned. Tonight Petye might finally learn just what was possible in the service of the Emperor. The man's last act of servitude. If he ever showed himself.

"Petye!"

Mournar crossed the dim room, ignoring a sharp pain in his right knee, refusing to limp. He opened the next set of doors and stepped out into the wide, towering, yet brilliantly-lit space beyond. The faintest noise echoed – his naked footsteps, the rustle of his robe – although there was over a moment's delay for each return, so vast was the mostly empty, vaulted void. Yet despite its size, everywhere was bright with a harsh radiance, cast by the wide shaft of sorcerous energy which rose silently through the centre of thousands of levels to this last floor: the apex of the tower city, Móce-Wieża. Capital of the Lęnj-Ńowić Empire. Raised by a wizard whose name was lost to history, forged from some unknown alloy which was probably sorcerous in nature, ancient even before the first Emperor, Romyzh, had claimed it for his home, centuries ago. Every floor was a sprawling, separate municipality with dwellings large and small, its own administration, businesses, parks, the upper levels growing smaller in area until the very highest were little more than grandiose estates for the empire's court and governing élite. The apex floor was solely for the Emperor, imperial staff and personal militia, with palaces, suites and barracks arranged around the central core of magic, under a steep, pyramidal roof.

Mournar looked around. Units of that very militia should be stationed about the place, patrolling, guarding his person. But he saw no one. The domes and towers of the many manses spread across the level were starkly lit by the harsh light, but all appeared deserted.

There was no movement – save for the occasional flicker within the shaft of sorcerous power. The entrance to his own palace – its tall gates flanked by towering, grotesque statuary, their bizarre sculpts made all the more sinister by the stark shadows cast by the tower's central light source – stood unguarded. Other than those thrown by his own movements, he heard not a single echo. The supporting shaft of light was, as ever, mute.

The sense of alarm he had felt on awakening returned. Where was everyone? Were they gathered elsewhere, plotting? Already poised to rise up? Was this the revolt he had expected and feared since the moment he had slain the previous Emperor and ascended to the imperial throne?

He turned about and ran back to his chamber as swiftly as he could – treacherous joints be damned! Once there he crossed the floor and closed his hands around Krysolac's hilt. The golden broadsword came away from its wall mounts easily, as if thirsting for destruction, its serpentine, flamberge blade seeming to dance in the lamplight. As Mournar raised the weapon it was as if all his aches and fears dissolved away. The sword's complex gold and silver filigree handguard appeared to shift slightly, settling around his hand in a lover's caress.

"Now!" he roared. "Now let them take the crown! Now let them try and unthrone me!"

He strode from his chamber, out through the dim outer room and into the gaudily-lit apex level. It was as silent and deserted as before.

"To me!" he yelled, awakening a chorus of slow, endless echoes, feeding off themselves. "To me!"

He walked forward, slowly, cautiously, his attention flickering about the vast level, alert for ambush. Nothing moved. He might have been alone in the entire tower-city.

The broad central shaft of nameless light burned mercilessly, silently, only the occasional flicker of darker light disturbing its otherwise featureless appearance. Each time the illumination flickered the shadows in the niches and corners of the ornate decoration about him danced momentarily, giving the illusion of furtive movement. Each time he raised Krysolac in nervous readiness, only to lower the sword moments later.

"Is this a game?" he called into the silence, stirring further echoes. "Be warned, Mournar of Móce-Wieża has no time for games!"

Once the echoes had died, only silence answered him.

To his right was the beginning of a curved ramp, one of many leading to the next level down. He paced towards it, moving sidewards, still alert for anything. Once on the ramp, one wide enough to take an entire cavalry unit, he began to follow it down, ever cautious, expecting an armed force to come screaming from where it lay in ambush, among the blind spots where the ramp spiralled down under the floor, towards the level far below. None came.

Once he had descended below the apex level – its floor now a high ceiling – Mournar paused, gazing down from the ramp's unrailed edge. The next level spread before him: a mosaic of many-storeyed administrative buildings; a river which ran a meandering course inside the tower's circumference, its surface a quicksilver mirror, ending where it began; ostentatious cathedrals dedicated to many gods, each attempting to surpass the others in splendour, size and piety; several market squares – all deserted. And enclosed by it all rose the searing backbone of Móce-Wieża, lighting everything with its harsh, actinic blaze.

Mournar squinted a moment as the vista before him blurred. A blink, two, and the panorama once more sharpened into better focus.

He glanced up the ramp again, to check that a company was not silently advancing towards him. The golden sword in his hand seemed to twitch, or was it just a tic in his arm. For a moment he thought he would continue down the curving ramp to the lower level, then decided against it. There was no reason for him to descend. What did he expect to find, except more deserted buildings?

Instead, he walked back up to the apex level, Krysolac raised in readiness. There was still no one to be seen when he reached the peak of the ramp, just a harshly-lit desolation. A suburb without people.

Mournar stood a while in silence, sweeping the deserted apex with his dark gaze. Móce-Wieża had a core population of almost two million, and the ramps were the only way between levels. It would take days to evacuate the tower, and the resultant noise would have raised constant echoes throughout the whole city. He could never have slept through that. No man could.

Unless he was drugged.

He thought back to the last food and drink he had eaten. Had there been an odd taste to it? A bitterness?

He shook his head. Trying to mould his memories to fit wild conspiracies was not the way. He could convince himself of anything by such a method.

But his dreams, though – dreams of screaming and shaking walls.

Had that been his slumbering mind, interpreting the tumult of a mass evacuation into something even more raucous?

Mournar's right arm twitched again and he rubbed at his shoulder muscles, trying to ease it.

His eyes were drawn towards the blazing shaft of sorcerous light, and where it was released through the apex of the tower. Outside, it terminated in an iridescent halo, dissipating in a multitude of rainbow hues Mournar could no more name than he could the colour of the tower's magical spine. From where he stood he could not see it, but behind that blazing shaft towered the great throne of Lęnj-Ńowić, high under the pyramidal roof. If there was an insurrection, the leader would certainly be there. Perhaps already declaring themselves the new Emperor, surrounded by fawning lackeys and opportunists. Feeling themselves safe while he, the anointed Emperor Mournar, lay drugged in his chamber, awaiting their final pleasure.

Mournar began to walk across the floor, the rub of his naked feet on the polished alloy finding an answer in reverberant murmurs. He was right. He had always been right. It was how he had risen through the ranks of the imperial armies: anticipation, always knowing what his enemies' moves would be, killing if he had to but finding subversion and coercion much more to his palate. Men's weaknesses were always the sharpest weapon. And with the unbreakable golden sword Krysolac at his side – its name supposedly meaning 'the Serpent' in some archaic Ńowizhan dialect – he could easily take what wasn't offered, however reluctantly.

The killing and various torments in which his inventive brain revelled came later, when his position was unassailable and he could enjoy such pleasant diversions just for themselves, rather than as a means.

His answers were to be found with the throne, as they had many decades ago. He was certain of it. As certain as he knew the smell of blood and shit.

Mournar broke into an easy jog. Circumventing the bright support shaft, he eventually reached the wide steps that led up to the imperial throne. Formed from the same unknown material as the rest of the tower-city, the steps flowed upwards, as if a portion of the floor had risen up to the tower's apex in a single fluid column before being moulded into a staircase. Two vast statues stood guard on either side of the steps, either of figures in finely decorated, strangely-shaped armour, or creatures that may have been monstrous birds. As Mournar understood it, they had been here as long as the tower had stood, and no one alive knew what they had originally been meant to portray.

Crumpled at the feet of one statue were two bodies. Mournar crouched to examine them, turning both over. The rattle as they were moved resounded all about the top level. They were members of his personal guard, in flamboyant blue and gold. There were no signs of injury, no rents in the fine armour, but both exposed faces looked shrunken and aged. Not everyone had fled, then. These two, at least, had died fighting ... something.

Mournar gazed up the towering flight of steps. Even though the magical column at his back flooded everywhere with its unforgiving light, the very top of the steps – the throne itself – was cloaked in shadow. A shadow that seemed to writhe and pulse. Mournar blinked his eyes again, cursing their weakness.

Taking Krysolac's hilt in a firmer grip, he stepped onto the first stair.

"Ah, Emperor Mournar. Finally. Welcome, your Imperial Majesty. Please, come ahead and join us." The voice seemed to come from all directions, yet there was no echo. It was deep, hypnotic, almost sensuous.

Mournar paused. "Who are you? Petye?" His own shout reverberated about the shaped roof, almost losing itself among its echoes. "General Kaychim?"

The voice laughed softly. *"We are legion, Emperor. Come – join us..."*

"Come down and face *me*!"

"When your throne is so comfortable? We do not think we will be vacating it quite so readily."

Mournar bit back his rage. An assault up the steps would normally be suicidal: whoever lurked in the shifting darkness had the high ground. Yet they clearly had no intention of yielding it. Why should they, now they had all the advantages.

And how many could there be? Under the apex was only the great imperial throne – the height of three men and the width of two – there was room for no more than one person at any time. All of the available space was occupied by a huge, black, crystalline chair.

Mournar sucked in a breath, Krysolac a reassuring weight in his hand. "Prepare to defend yourself!" he called. His only answer was taunting echoes.

He climbed steadily, looking about with each step, his ears

straining for the least sound of ambush: the creak of a bow, a careless scrape of steel. All he heard were the faint reverberations of his own footsteps. When he judged himself to be halfway up he paused, looking back down at the floor – so far below him. Other than the dead guardsmen, their bodies highlighted by stark shadows, there was still no one to be seen. This level – and by extension, perhaps the entire city – continued to appear deserted.

He looked up towards the tower's zenith. There was still nothing to be made out other than the crawling darkness. Mournar wished he had a pistol or arquebus to accompany his sword – a lead ball fired into that murk would make him feel better, and certainly chip away some confidence from whoever awaited him.

Unless they had a musket of their own, already trained on his body.

He dismissed the thought. If that were so they could have shot him easily enough before he had climbed so far.

He resumed his ascent.

The bright illumination from the tower's support column seemed to be flickering once more. Shadows danced in the carved niches of the giant statues flanking him, giving an illusion of staccato movement.

The dimness above him still moved with a life of its own – or was it an illusion created by the vast light source behind him as it flickered spasmodically.

Mournar paused again, looking over his shoulder at the tower's magical support. Flecks of darkness arose from where it emerged through the floor below, flickered past and up into the apex like shreds of wispy cloud driven by a storm. The Emperor frowned, for the first time wondering what was happening to the shaft of energy. Was it failing after who knew how many centuries? If so, how long would Móce-Wieża stand? Was this the reason everyone had fled? Had they known, and left him to die when the tower-city eventually fell? While he chased some apparition to that tower's highest point?

Mournar was no coward, but he knew the value of retreat when called for. Dying pointlessly was for poems and epics.

"Have no fear, little Mournar – Móce-Wieża will stand yet."

The taunting voice pricked his anger. For a moment he thought his golden broadsword actually tugged at his hand, urging him up the final steps. He grinned ferociously, baring his long, sharp canines. The city would stand. Long enough, at least.

He sprinted up the final steps. Before him, the shifting darkness resolved itself into a more solid shape. Something slumped in the huge, glittering bulk of the black throne. Something that changed its shape constantly, its limbs, head and torso shifting between animal, plant, and less identifiable forms, always mismatched. Sometimes transforming so gradually it was hard to discern the actual change, sometimes so swiftly it made Mournar's head pound. Clutched in a limb that one moment was a green frond, the next a birdlike talon, the next something vaguely insectoid was a tall black staff, tipped in a metal that was neither golden nor silvery, but something of both. It glinted in the light of Móce-Wieża's support column.

That shaft of magical force touched the tower's apex not a spear's length from the top of the staff, and strands of it bled out of the bright column, wrapping themselves around the top of the staff. With each thin eruption, the column of light momentarily dimmed, and the staff's tip grew brighter.

The ever-changing shape tilted a reptilian head in Mournar's direction, huge, compound eyes glittering. It opened tooth-edged jaws in a wide grin.

"Welcome, Imperial Majesty. We are Shilnoth – called the Shapeless, sometimes the Many-Shaped. We are sure you can appreciate why." The calm, hypnotic voice altered in pitch and timbre as the thing changed shape. And still it failed to cause a single echo.

"I call you cold meat." Mournar raised Krysolac, ready to carve the amorphous thing into gobbets. The staff was lowered a fraction, not quite in a parry. Mournar's sword halted in its swing as though it had impacted on something unbelievably solid and impenetrable, even though the blade was over an arm's length from the staff. Shock ran up Mournar's arm, partly numbing it.

"Your blade has more wisdom than you, Emperor. Even a Sword of Fate will fare poorly against this staff, lately come into our possession. A *mandra'al*, able to spin the warp and weft of the Boundless about itself, and more than a match for any bodkin." A grin that was all teeth leered at Mournar, before it collapsed in on itself and briefly goggled back like a huge fish.

Mournar spat in response, took a two-handed grip on his sword, and thrust hard at that gaping face. Again Shilnoth barely twitched the staff, and Krysolac seemed to smash into an impassable wall. This time the shock of the impact numbed both of Mournar's arms.

"Play this game as long as you wish, semi-mortal," sighed Shilnoth, his expression that of some kind of shaggy, morose dog. "It will take us time to drain the power of this remarkable city's support column.

During which the *mandra'al* – and by extension ourself – will grow only stronger. All future attempts to assault us will only become increasingly painful. For you, at least."

Mournar lowered his golden broadsword. He would wait until the tingle had left his limbs before he tried again. "You said semi-mortal."

Shilnoth laughed, although the shape perched atop his shoulders seemed to be howling in anguish. "Your appearance, Emperor, tells us much. The feral teeth, the long, sharp lobeless ears, your features which – even we can tell – are uncommonly fair for a human. There is the mark of a Celestial about you." He leaned forward, or his form shifted so that it flowed closer to the Emperor, examining him as though he was some fascinating specimen. "Your sire, we would imagine. There are many Eternals who seem to delight in savouring the various pleasures afforded by mortal flesh. We have always thought such diversions to be ... deviant."

"I did not know my father..."

"A not uncommon situation with mortals, as we understand it. But did your mother never speak of the one who sired you? Of the unbearable pleasure she would have endured throughout the coupling?"

"She died in childbirth..."

"Also often the case. Be grateful the coupling itself did not destroy her."

The black staff trembled for a moment. Curlicues of bright energy spiralling from the magical column's apex spun about it. Shilnoth groaned with something approaching ecstasy, as his constantly shifting form shuddered.

"Ahhhhhh—! *This* is true pleasure – not that momentary titillation briefly sensed while rutting with some short-lived beast! Soon we shall be ready. Then all that is required is your sword."

Mournar gripped Krysolac tighter. "I will never yield it – not even to a … whatever you are."

"We are the Boundless Incarnate, semi-mortal. Infinite in variety and form, endless in complexity." A face that was almost human smiled momentarily from atop a bobbing stalk. "Or at least, so we like to believe." He waved a limb crystallising into jagged blue teeth at the level below them. "Did you know this tower was conceived as a sort of representation of the Boundless: Tier upon Tier, realms stacked over realms. The wizard who constructed it – quite literally pouring his soul into it—" his staff pointed towards the flickering central column "—was ambitious, but unimaginative, and understood little of reality's paradoxes. At least he has been able – in a way – to enjoy his folly these past centuries. Until we bring it all down, of course…"

Shilnoth came slowly to his feet, or his endlessly reshaping form transmuted from a sitting to a standing shape. Mournar found it hard to be sure. The creature's constantly flowing shape was hypnotic.

The Emperor shook his head and took a backward step down the stairs. Above him Shilnoth mirrored his actions: a lower limb, shaped into an insect's articulated leg, coming down hard on the top step. The black staff was held high, the swirling accumulation of magic from the tower's draining support column growing ever brighter.

Mournar raised Krysolac. It seemed to tremble in his hands.

Shilnoth chuckled, a huge beak snapping shut before it was reabsorbed. "We do believe your sword is afraid, little Emperor." He levelled his staff and its pulsing cloud of growing magical power, directly at Mournar. "And so it should be."

The Emperor retreated another step, silently cursing himself. When had he ever backed away from an enemy? He was the Emperor Mournar, feared throughout the Lęnj-Ńowić Empire almost as much as his golden sword. A sword which had never failed him, never lost its edge, always defended him against any number of foes. Yet, did it now sense weakness as age overcame him, as it must? He had borne Krysolac for thirty years, ten times that of any of the weapon's previous owners. Boryden Ceńawić, who Mournar had killed to take Krysolac for himself, had carried the golden sword for less than two years; the previous, unnamed owner for five. Bearing Krysolac had never been a guarantee of a long life, yet he – Mournar the Demonic – had done so for three decades. He was fated.

As if to underline his thoughts he felt a gentle squeeze about his right hand. Reassurance. Above all others, Krysolac favoured him.

Mournar laughed himself, throwing it in the shifting face of the thing above him. The Emperor stood taller, sucking in a deep breath, and raised the golden broadsword.

"By this blade I rule," he said, low and calm. Few echoes followed his words. "For half a lifetime I have ruled the empire, crushing any who sought to defy me – man or province. As I will do now, though my foe be something from the deepest hells and the world fall about me."

Shilnoth tilted a writhing knot of tendrils where his head should have been. "Brave words. No doubt the kind of empty rhetoric with which you have inspired your allies and unmanned your enemies ever since ascending to the throne behind us. And prophetic – for indeed your world is about to shatter and fall."

He swung his staff. Traceries of burning power followed it in an arc. For a moment the great shaft holding the tower of Móce-Wieża upright blinked out, plunging them into utter darkness. Mournar felt a shudder under his feet, and a deep, almost subaural groan rolled up from the city's base, so many levels below him.

The light flickered back again, in time for Mournar to see the black staff slashing down at his head. He dropped to one knee, and the staff's tip swept past, just grazing his right shoulder. Even so the pain was intense, momentarily overwhelming, though it faded swiftly.

He stood, braced with one foot on a lower step, as Shilnoth brought his staff upright again. He wielded the weapon awkwardly, Mournar noted, as much due to the ever-changing shape of the limbs holding it as inexperience, he thought.

"Impressive," spoke the shapeless thing. "Although you cannot dodge us indefinitely."

"That is not my intention. One thrust of my sword is all I need."

"Ironically, on that we are agreed."

Shilnoth spun his staff and lashed at Mournar once more. As the Emperor dodged the blow he felt Krysolac stir in his hand. The sword seemed to rise of its own volition, ready to parry the staff – then fell meekly at his side.

"Interesting," said Shilnoth as he once again grounded his staff. "The sword seems conflicted – unsure whether to shield you or protect itself."

"You speak as though it were alive." Although Mournar had

himself sometimes half-thought that to be so. How many times had Krysolac parried a blow he had barely been aware of, or executed a cunning thrust to finish an opponent? Moves the Emperor had told himself were simply the result of many years' practice and unconscious skill.

"Sentient, certainly." Shilnoth raised the staff again, and Mournar tensed. Instead of a blow, the silver-gold tip drank more deeply of the flickering energies that now danced erratically up the tower's spine. The light dimmed but did not go out. Dazzling sprites whirled along the staff's length, hiding Shilnoth behind their bright display. "And parasitic. Why do you think the lives of every wielder have been so short?"

"They died as they lived," said Mournar. "And my life has not been so brief."

"Only because of your Celestial heritage." Shilnoth's voice now came from behind an almost solid beam of light: the tower-city's backbone in miniature. "It had a much deeper well from which to drink. Even so, we imagine you feel some weakness, some frailty..."

"The afflictions of age..."

"A half mortal mongrel such as you should feel no such afflictions – not for many centuries. Were it not for that gilded leech you might be all but immortal."

Mournar laughed again. "And you wish it for yourself? You lie—!"

"Our need is but for a brief span of time. Once we have accomplished that, the sword will be free to seek another host."

Mournar staggered for a moment as the stairs on which he stood shuddered. "Forgive me if I do not believe you."

"Your belief is of no matter to us, one way or another."

All about Mournar the apex level grew dim as the once blazing column supporting the tower faded by degrees. With each cascading flicker the brilliance died, while the staff clutched in Shilnoth's unstable grasp grew brighter by the same measure. The Emperor would have charged up the steps, swinging Krysolac in a last, desperate foray, but he was held back. His confidence seemed to be ebbing with the light. Never before had he known such doubt.

He raised his sword. In the uncertain illumination its serpentine length seemed to be writhing impatiently. Its golden colour was muted, almost an identical hue to the silver-gold tips of Shilnoth's black staff.

"All this time," he said, a bitter understanding coming to him, "it has been the sword. My rise through the ranks, carving my way up until I finally sat upon the imperial throne, all the while shielded by Krysolac – as I thought – saved by it more times than I remember. Yet it was not I who wielded it. Rather, it wielded me as a blunt instrument; goading my ambition so that it might ride my success. And for its own, unfathomable reasons!" He felt unbearably tired and remembered what Shilnoth had said earlier. "Even as it fed on me..."

For the first time he looked at the golden broadsword, its elaborate basket hilt and flamberge blade, without pride and admiration. Instead, something like revulsion filled him.

"Then I have no further use for you," he spat at the sword.

The winding hilt tightened about his hand, squeezing harder until Mournar thought his bones would crush. He cried out – then used the pain to fuel his anger. He gave way to it, enjoying the surrender as an almost uncontrollable fury flooded his veins.

He swung the broadsword, oblivious to the crushing pain in his hand, the agonising jolt as Krysolac tried to hold back his assault. He fed on his rage, allowing it to overcome his fatigue and pain, enjoying the abandon as he battered again and again at a suddenly retreating Shilnoth.

The shapeless creature blocked each of Mournar's reckless blows with his staff, his movements as lacking in finesse as the Emperor's. There was no skill in this duel, only wild desperation and senseless determination. Each time blade and staff connected there was a deafening toll, and endless echoes which tripped over each other. Each time Mournar felt as though he was striking against the very tower of Móce-Wieża itself. His hands were numb, beyond pain; his body screamed with exertion and dripped sweat. He no longer felt anything beyond a desire to cut through the black staff, and shatter his golden sword as he did so. Destroy them both.

The stairs shuddered once more, collapsing by more than a man's height. Mournar fell, stretching out across several twisted steps. Ribs snapped, but he barely noticed. On either side the towering statues twisted inward, as though they were gazing down on the prostrate Emperor with baffled interest.

Mournar propped himself up, using Krysolac as a crutch. The stairs above were twisted and unsafe. Nevertheless, Shilnoth was picking his way down them, his ever-morphing shape peculiarly suited to the crumbling steps. His staff blazed with writhing light, casting uneasy shadows which found a match in the echoes still resounding about the tower's tilted apex.

"You have some merit," said the shapeless one. "A certain courage. We wish we could take you with us, along with those citizens of Móce-Wieża who did not die in your defence – not that you have yet to show any interest in them. Another admirable quality. Them we have a use for. However, your life is part of the bargain – we are sure you must expect that."

"The previous owner of Krysolac must die at the hands of the next..." It was something Mournar had always presumed, although it was never spoken of.

"Some of the Swords of Fate seem to prefer it that way." Shilnoth was now almost an arm's length away. Mournar tried to lever himself to his feet, but his fury was gone, along with much of his strength. Krysolac no longer held his hand in a crushing grip and seemed to be trying to slip from his grasp. "It is not a requirement as we understand it – although we will do our best to honour the pact. More a peculiarity in the blades' temperaments."

Shilnoth now stood directly over Mournar. The Emperor made one last attempt to rise, but Krysolac wriggled free and he lost his balance, half-sprawling across the collapsed staircase. Shilnoth's staff stabbed down.

The energy of a colourless sun erupted around Mournar. He would have screamed, but his jaw and half his face were melted into a solid lump in the first second. He felt his skin sear and crisp, blowing away in the blast. His limbs knotted and twisted, his body curled in on itself, huddling in an attempt to escape the agony.

It was over in moments that felt like an eternity. Mournar lay on the steps, parts of him burnt, parts of him still bloody, and parts nothing but raw pain. Somehow he could still see, partially, although his eyes must surely be boiled away. The staff still blazed with unnameable light, while the column holding up Móce-Wieża was almost extinguished.

Shilnoth bent over him, several green tendrils sprouting down to wrap themselves around Krysolac. He raised the sword and aimed the point at Mournar.

"Shall we say this is a merciful stroke, although neither of us believes in such a concept."

He thrust the blade home. Mournar felt it as an impossibly cold skewer freezing his bowels.

Shilnoth flowed upright, his image fading with the light, or Mournar's vision. A moment later all was blackness.

As consciousness fled, Mournar felt the first tremors of an ancient tower's death throes.

89

WHERE THE SUN HAS NEVER SHONE

FOR A MOMENT the dawn air was punctuated by the clash of steel. Then silence fell again, leaving an uneasy quiet.

Backed against a tall stone wall stood two figures, swords raised against five in outlandish yellow and grey armour, all holding bared scimitars. Their stances were threatening, but none seemed willing to step closer to the pair. Three of their number already lay on the scuffed brittle grass, armour split, slowly expanding pools of blood steaming in the cold air.

One of the cornered pair was a tall man all in black, from his flared trousers to his wide-sleeved, laced and ribboned blouse. His mane of long hair was of the same colour, as were his roguish beard and the pair of twinkling eyes set in a dark, handsome face. Even the blade of his basket-hilted sword was black, and in the reddish dawn light it seemed to emit a deep, smoky glow.

The second figure was in stark contrast. A gleaming gold and crimson helm covered his head, fashioned in the shape of a screaming bird of prey. His clothing was no less remarkable, and in the gaudiest of colours: a lavender and rich green doublet, its sleeves slashed and puffed over a loose yellow shirt, scarlet britches laced below the knee and tucked into high-topped brown boots. All were stained and dusty. His sword was the colour of fresh blood, and its blade was split from the point to halfway along its length: twin tines which hummed discordant notes as it was swung.

The man in black grinned, twirling his sword point in an extravagant pattern. "Come now. Five against two. Did our good fortune with your comrades unman you all? Perhaps you'll have better luck."

For a moment longer the standoff continued. Then, as though at a covert signal between the armoured five, all attacked at once.

Two came at the man in black. They hacked at him with their scimitars. He evaded both swords, his own riposting in a dark blur. One assailant fell back with a cry, clutching at a sword arm that was suddenly half its length. The second danced aside, his armour deflecting the blow. He swung his scimitar, aiming for the other's midriff. The black sword caught the swing, its blade ringing like an angry bell. A twist, and the armoured man was left defenceless – his sword landing a yard to his left. The man in black lunged, driving his own sword between gorget and breastplate.

The remaining three descended upon the second, flamboyant figure, confident of their victory. One cut at his left arm. The red sword darted, catching the scimitar blade between its twin points, snatching it from the assailant's grasp. A flick of the red blade and the scimitar spun into the air – to be caught by the garish figure's free hand.

"Two for two." Despite the strange helm, its wearer's deep voice came through clearly. He raised both swords. When the two armed men struck – one to the left, one to the right – the scimitar blocked one blade, while the red sword flickered below the second and cut through its wielder's breastplate as though it was old parchment. The armoured man sank to the ground. The flamboyant figure pivoted, slashing at the last armoured man. He backed, stumbling over a fallen body. The one in the screaming bird helm danced forward, shearing through the other's grotesque armour with the twin-pointed blade. They died silently.

The duo straightened, surveying the field of battle. Six lay dead or dying, one knelt on the churned grass, vainly trying to staunch the blood gushing from his half an arm, the eighth was backing away. A moment later he fled towards a veranda on the sprawling building several yards away. Both men lowered their weapons. The one in the bird helm threw the scimitar aside. It stuck in the ground, quivering.

"Well, my friend," said the man in black with a wide grin, "I think we've earned our absence from this place."

The other reached up and removed the gold and crimson helm.

From it emerged a narrow, boyish face so smooth and pale it could have been carved from alabaster. Long curling hair of a vivid orange fell around it. His eyes were entirely red, with no whites, and the black pupils were narrow, horizontal slits. He squinted, as though even the pale dawn light was too harsh. Around his eyes and down his cheeks ran a complex series of angular, black tattoos, stark against his colourless skin.

The man in black sheathed his sword and glanced at his comrade-in-arms with some surprise. "You're from Vainë-kyuni." His tone implied the pale-skinned figure had no business being anywhere else.

The orange-haired man paused, his own sword halfway to its sheath. "You are the first in this dismal land to have ever heard of my home." Freed of the helm, there was a clear, if faint, accent to his voice. He slammed his sword home. "I am Gaijori Akkanëyodi—"

"—Of the clan Kanëyo. I recognise the family tattoos. You're a long way from home, Gaijori Akkanëyodi."

The other stared for a moment. "You speak as though you have visited Vainë-kyuni – except that is impossible. Its shores are sealed to all outsiders."

The man in black's grin grew wider. "Nothing is impossible, Gaijori – may I call you that? – at least not to some of us." He performed a deep, courtly bow, sweeping out his left arm in salute, as though it clutched a fine hat. "Aundrém. Aundrém of ... everywhere. And nowhere."

"Indeed?" Gaijori tucked his helm below his left arm. "So how did you find yourself in this particular hell?" He nodded towards the distant sprawl of a building.

Aundrém followed his gaze. "Hmm? Ah – I made the mistake of voicing my opinion that after Móce-Wieża's long overdue collapse into a pile of rubble – taking with it the barely lamented emperor – the moribund Lęnj-Ńowić Empire is little more than a walking corpse blighting Ažen's landscape. All within earshot of a couple of Graav Illyć Vandersaan's men. These ancient nobles are very proud of their walking corpse, it seems. He took the criticism hard." The man rubbed at his jaw, expression rueful.

"He wanted me for his menagerie. Plus my mount." The anger was raw in Gaijori's voice. "Like two exotic pets."

"You have a Vainë-kyuni horse?" Aundrém shook his head. "My friend, I'm surprised you weren't killed or enslaved the moment you stepped off—"

He was interrupted by a wild shout. Both men turned. A tall but withered figure was hobbling towards them from the veranda. The once fine clothing swamping his gaunt frame was faded, as colourless as the strands of hair stuck to his flaking skull. The thick whitening smeared across his face could not disguise the pockmarked skin; nor the ludicrous number of beauty spots detract from many dark tumours. He was leaning heavily on a scuffed matchlock arquebus, using it as a crutch. Smoke trickled from the lit match held in its serpentine.

"Graav Vandersaan," said Aundrém lightly. "Come to bid us farewell?" His hand rested on his sword hilt.

"Deviants!" the old man coughed. "You will not leave. You are mine...!"

He halted, seizing the barrel of the arquebus in thin, gnarled hands. The matchlock slipped through his grasp and fell to the ground. The serpentine holding the match fell, touching the powder. A second later the weapon roared. A chunk of the wall, a yard to the right of Gaijori's head, crumbled. Somewhat belatedly, the Vainë-kyuni ducked.

Aundrém took a step forward. He raised his hand, but didn't draw his sword. The ancient Graav half-stumbled, groping for the discharged, now useless arquebus.

"Vandersaan!"

The old man looked up at the sound of Aundrém's voice. There was bright light playing around the man in black's right hand: a score of sprites chasing each other in endless pulsing circles. The light grew more dazzling with each strobe. Gaijori squinted his all-red eyes, almost closing them altogether.

"I neglected to thank you for your hospitality, Graav," said Aundrém, his tone playful. "Very remiss of me."

A dazzling bolt spewed from his raised hand. It struck Vandersaan. The old man screamed, but the cry was cut short. His hunched body was engulfed in brilliant white fire. It burned for several seconds, and when the flames died there was little remaining – save for a few stinking embers which blew away on a cold breeze.

Aundrém glanced towards the building. At a gesture it flew apart, stones erupting, splinters of veranda scattering violently across the sparse grass. All that remained was smoking dust.

He lowered his hand, a pained grimace etched on his face. He turned to Gaijori, the grimace relaxing into a sad smile.

"Farewells made, my friend. Now, show me your Vainë-kyuni

mount – I've not seen one of your horned horses in many a year!"

❦ ❦ ❦

MIDDAY FOUND THEM riding down a raised flint road between fields of maize which seemed to stretch on to infinity in every direction. Pale houses and workers' huts dotted the waving landscape like imperfections, each one dead and empty now that the growing season was over. Unshuttered windows stared blindly, like empty sockets.

Aundrém sat astride a stolen black pony – he clearly had a liking for that hue – which continuously shied away from Gaijori's own mount: a tall maroon creature which closely resembled a horse, save for its sharp beak, clawed split hooves, and a set of magnificently curled horns growing from its long skull. A wild-tempered Vainë-kyuni horse which had saved him more than once since arriving on this strange continent.

It was a year or more since he had left Vainë-kyuni, crossing an unnamed ocean to find Ažen – an all but forgotten myth in his homeland. Months of aimless wandering in which he had learned to master their guttural tongue, although his fluency had not lessened the fear, disgust, loathing and hatred he encountered. Then imprisonment in Vandersaan's menagerie. He would have been there still if fate hadn't introduced his present companion, attempting an escape at the same time as Gaijori. The Vainë-kyuni doubted he would have made it alone – even against the Graav's untrained and unskilled guards. They had numbers on their side, after all.

And it was clear Aundrém was a sorcerer of sorts. A powerful one.

The thought made Gaijori wary. Vainë-kyuni had legends of a caste of sorcerers who had once ruled the land: vain, capricious, notoriously cruel. In children's stories one avoided them at all costs, or suffered for it.

Yet Aundrém seemed amiable enough – even if he was in love with his own voice. A morning listening to his endless prattle had felt like an eternity. In Gaijori's experience one who talked so much had either nothing to say, or was deliberately saying nothing.

Aundrém finished winding the spring on the second of a brace of wheellock pistols. He slid it into a pommel holster hanging off his pony's saddle and rubbed at his dark beard with dusty black gloves Gaijori did not remember him donning. His expression was wry.

"There's nothing more depressing than an agricultural area in winter, my friend," he remarked.

"Do you not enjoy the sun?" asked Gaijori. He found it painful. Even the wan light of a presently overcast sun was a little too bright for eyes accustomed to permanently thunderous Vainë-kyuni skies. He didn't think he would ever get used to white clouds.

The man in black peered at the half-clouded sky, and the presently hidden sun. "Small comfort," he muttered. "Or perhaps it's just hunger talking."

He reached into a saddlebag and drew out two large pies. He tossed one to Gaijori, taking a deep bite out of his own. After a few moments' chewing he swallowed and shook his head. "No – it's most definitely the winter..."

Gaijori looked at the heavy pasty in his hands, sniffing it suspiciously. Where exactly had it come from? He was certain there had been no bags on the pony when Aundrém stole it. He took a cautious bite. It was packed with spicy, unrecognisable meat, and was quite delicious. He ate it quickly.

"You have implied several times that you know Vainë-kyuni," he said, voicing a thought which had bothered him all morning. "Yet the land has always been sealed to outsiders by the most potent magic. Most believe there is nothing beyond our shores except an infinite black ocean."

Aundrém laughed quietly. "While I might wonder how you came by such a unique sword."

Gaijori unconsciously glanced down. "It is a family heirloom, handed down to the eldest son..."

Aundrém gave him a frank look. "A status I have the feeling you don't deserve."

Gaijori bridled. "I am the youngest of four. When I announced my intention to voyage beyond Vainë-kyuni I was mocked – so I went anyway."

"And stole the sword."

"Borrowed. I shall return it."

"Of course you will." Aundrém's grin was lopsided. "You made an excellent choice, though. I'm sure you've noticed how the edge never dulls and it can slice through any armour."

Gaijori had, many times. "No more so than your own sword."

Aundrém bowed his head in acknowledgement. "Hardly surprising – they are cousins, as it were. Have you heard of the Swords of Fate? In Vainë-kyuni they may go by another name."

Gaijori thought for a moment. "The *Burikkydë-nusori*? The six-bladed Sword of Providence...?"

Aundrém shrugged. "As you say. Imagine then what you wear at your waist is one of those blades, operating independently." He patted his sword hilt. "And this is another."

Gaijori laughed. "And of course I am a warrior, chosen by fate to wield it."

"Laugh all you want, my friend. The Swords select who they wish to bear them, not the other way around. I have worn Durandor for many years, on and off, and never at my own choice."

"Indeed?" Gaijori tried to keep the disbelief from his voice. He was a little old for such tales.

Aundrém shrugged again. "I merely advise you. Believe me or not."

"It also has a name, I suppose?"

"Naturally. This—" he patted his sword's basket hilt "—is Durandor – or so it is known in this corner of the Boundless, at least. And the red blade is Sangrinn."

Aundrém looked so serious that Gaijori was almost tempted to believe him. And that term he used – the Boundless – it was familiar, somehow... "Well, you have entertained me with that tale – now amuse me further by explaining how you know my homeland so well."

Aundrém's black eyes twinkled. "My friend, I can travel the infinite Tiers of the Internection. Do you think a few magical wards would stop me?"

He raised an arm and made a sweeping head to saddle gesture. His form shimmered. His face grew pallid, black hair fading to a yellow so pale it was almost colourless. His eyes became a glowing orange. The black clothes morphed into robes so rich and vibrant that Gaijori's dusty finery looked drab and vulgar. Even the pony was now a deep purple Vainë-kyuni horse, its flanks level with Gaijori's head, its magnificent horns stretching over three feet, tip to tip.

"Well, Gaijori Akkanëyodi of the clan Kanëyo?" He spoke High Kyu fluently, better than Gaijori. "Dost thou think I might pass amongst thy brethren unchallenged?" Another gesture and the illusion drifted away like mist on a hot day. Aundrém was smiling, somewhat self-consciously. "Apologies. I can never resist that parlour trick."

At that moment Gaijori remembered where he had heard of the Boundless: as a child. Stories of the endless realms stacked and clustered beyond this one, populated by gods and monsters, creatures of evil masquerading as good, and vice versa. The many worlds were sometimes referred to with a Low Kyu term which could translate as levels, or tiers. It was where the fearful sorcerers who had supposedly ruled Vainë-kyuni had fled to, or come from; the tales were typically vague on many points. When he reached adulthood Gaijori had discarded such fables, considering them crude metaphors, or another way of saying far, far away. Now this Aundrém spoke as if it were all true. If he were not mad – and Gaijori could see no other evidence of madness – was this not one of the reasons he had left home? To search out the myths and wonders of the world?

He realised Aundrém was still talking, indicating the countryside with grandiose gestures.

"...You may think this landscape quite strange, with its blue skies and green hills – whilst those from Ažen, for example, would consider Vainë-kyuni to be positively nightmarish – yet there are realms within the Infinite Tiers that are far more delightful or lurid. Depending on your personal taste, of course. Forests of mist, floating seas that have sentient islands dangling from them, deserts of burning ice – anything you may imagine, and much that you cannot."

"Indeed?"

"It is the nature of infinite variety, my friend. The Boundless contains an infinite number of universes: the Tiers; although that term suggests a level of organisation which I have never found. Subtract an infinite number from an infinite number – and you will still have an infinite number remaining. An infinite number of Tiers swarming with life; an infinite number containing intelligent creatures resembling such as you and I; an infinite number wherein the intelligent life is far, far different; an infinite number that are the realms of immortals, referring to themselves as Eternals, or Celestials, but to mortals they would simply be gods, or demons – the difference is often negligible. And an infinite number where no manner of life exists, neither mortal nor immortal – not even the smallest, humblest animalcule."

Gaijori shook his head, finding the concepts too vast, too alarming.

"There are Tiers where gods hold sway, and Tiers where gods have never existed." Aundrém was clearly warming to his subject. "I have even heard it speculated that, if all is possible within the Boundless, then it must follow there are Tiers where the Internection itself does not exist, replaced by something else. Something stranger." He turned to face Gaijori, a wide smile across his handsome face. "But I think only a god could understand or explain that particular paradox."

"And neither of us are gods," Gaijori remarked, his tone wry.

Aundrém laughed. "Remember, my friend: all things are possible."

"And you claim to be able to transverse these Tiers at will?"

"More than a claim. I may transition to any level. Although—" his smile faded a little and his voice grew wistful "—there are Tiers – sometimes a great many, clustered in forgotten niches of the Internection – which are all but inaccessible. Sealed off for some reason or another – by the Source, the Boundless itself. Sometimes by its own inhabitants—"

His voice faltered, and for an instant Gaijori thought he detected a deep sadness in the man's black eyes. Then the moment was gone: the wide grin and twinkling gaze returned.

"I grow maudlin," laughed Aundrém. "And that will—" He reined in his pony abruptly, falling silent. His attention was fixed upon something across an endless field of old maize to his left. "Now what's that?" he murmured.

"Where?" The Vainë-kyuni squinted but saw nothing. He wondered if the other was simply attempting to change the conversation, embarrassed by a momentary show of emotion.

"That flashing." Aundrém pointed.

Gaijori shielded his eyes, and saw it. A rainbow flickering, far away among the maize stalks. It reminded him of marsh gas, but no natural phenomena could explain the unearthly beauty, or its bizarre mix of colour.

Aundrém urged his pony off the flint road and into the whispering cornstalks. After a pause Gaijori spurred his own maroon horse forward and followed Aundrém into the waving, hissing sea.

The pony whinnied and shied, eager to turn back. The horned Vainë-kyuni horse was more stoical; even so, its nostrils flared.

Neither animal cared for whatever was ahead. Aundrém himself was unusually silent, wrapped in thought, checking his mount's wayward lurches with practiced ease.

They emerged into a broad patch of roughly trampled, shredded maize. The dancing light hung over them, dazzling yet silent. It cast a moving illumination, throwing oddly coloured shadows which writhed and danced. Gaijori's weak eyes struggled to make out details in the treacherous light, and he shaded them as best he could.

A huge form lay crushed and obviously dead amid the flattened stalks. Oily sap glinted on an iridescent hide. Leaves stuck to it, a grotesque parody of feathers.

They tried to ride closer, but even Gaijori's horse refused to approach. Both men dismounted, drawing their swords. They advanced on the huge corpse, Gaijori wondering just what could have killed so large a creature, and fearful it might still be about.

Even on its side it was almost Gaijori's height. Its skin was covered in thick scales the size of his hand. Although slowly losing their lustre, the scales bore a sheen reminiscent of a rainbow. It had four upper limbs, and two heavy, reptilian hind legs. Its hammer-shaped head had no mouth, while two multi-faceted eyes bulged on either side. They were as cold and unseeing as jewels. Gaijori stared at the dead creature. There was something disturbingly familiar about it, some dreamlike memory.

"Qrymh."

Gaijori was startled by Aundrém's voice in the silence. "What?"

"Qrymh. One of nine sorcerers who once ruled ... a far off land. He and his sister quarrelled with them, millennia ago. They fled before the remaining seven could destroy them."

Gaijori stared at the dead thing. *"That* was a sorcerer?"

"Once he looked human. Gradually, his appearance was remodelled by his nature." Aundrém stepped closer and tapped the corpse with the tip of his boot. "Qryvi would not be unlike him now, I imagine." He sighed. "She was such a beauty..."

"You would know, of course."

"Yes." The sudden grief in Aundrém's eyes was so deep, Gaijori instantly regretted his mockery. The man in black sheathed his sword, shifting his gaze up to the cloudy sky. "Qryvi must be near, she was rarely parted from her brother."

As though in response, the overhead display erupted into a searing flash. Gaijori's vision was overwhelmed. Through tear-choked eyes he could just make out the small, blue-white sun come to life, skimming the cornstalk sea. In its wake it left a shrivelled and wilted trail wide enough for a platoon of infantry.

"Qrymh's essence!" said Aundrém. "He'll try and unite with Qryvi before it's spent. Quickly!"

He ran to his skittish pony. Vaulting into the saddle he impatiently motioned Gaijori to follow. A moment later the pony was sprinting away, fuelled by its nervous energy. Gaijori blinked away his tears and was in his saddle and following within seconds. He gave his mount its head, letting it speed through the seared maize, following the swooping light as though it was a beacon.

After a timeless gallop during which the fields rolled by, unchanging, a low range of hills appeared. Qrymh's life-essence was clearly headed for them.

The fields gave way to shallow, gravelly slopes. The horses left the maize behind, climbing into the hills. They were small affairs, covered in tough wiry grass and the bare trunks of stunted deciduous trees, or an occasional conifer.

The scintillating light vanished abruptly. The men reined in, staring up the slope.

Aundrém pointed. "Look! A cave, or tunnel."

Gaijori could just make out a mark on the hillside: a ragged hole part-hidden by a fall of rocks.

They urged their horses forward. Reaching the rockfall, they dismounted and looked the entrance over. It was a narrow slash in the hillside, just high enough for a riderless horse to duck through. A faint, indefinable odour wafted out of the darkness.

"Well?" asked Aundrém. "Do we continue?"

"Why not?" Gaijori was once more fired with the recklessness which had urged him to leave Vainë-kyuni, so long ago. "After coming this far."

Taking their horses' reins they stepped towards the mouth. Both animals baulked, refusing to take one step nearer to the cave. The Vainë-kyuni horse's yellow eyes glared, its nostrils flaring. Gaijori had never known it so distressed.

Aundrém shrugged. "Alone then."

They tethered their animals to the jagged branches of a gnarled hawthorn several paces back from the entrance. Aundrém lifted the pommel holster off his pony's saddle and slung it over his left shoulder. Gaijori unslung his helm from his own mount's high saddle.

They stepped into darkness.

As the light from the entrance faded, the rocky floor dropped abruptly away. Gaijori almost fell. Aundrém grabbed his shoulder as he stumbled. Stones slid and echoed down into the darkness.

"We'll need a torch," muttered Gaijori, getting back on his feet. Somehow, he was still holding onto his raptor helm. Even his vision, adapted as it was to permanent twilight, couldn't pierce the gloom.

Aundrém chuckled. There was a spark, a flare, and he was holding two dancing columns of flame. He handed a torch to Gaijori with a wink. The Vainë-kyuni took it, warily.

Aundrém led the descent. The last glimmer of light from the entrance cut off abruptly; only the flickering torches lit their way. Gaijori wondered where they were heading. At first, he had assumed the opening led to a deep cave, or a passage through the hill, but they were descending constantly. He grew anxious, his imagination populating the dancing shadows cast by the torches with strange shapes. Then one of the shadows scuttled into the light on multiple legs, and was as quickly gone.

Gaijori donned his helm, transferred torch to left hand, and drew his blood red sword without thinking. Its twin points hummed mournfully. Aundrém paused, turning, alerted by the sound. For a moment whatever Gaijori had seen rattled through the twin pools of light again, heading back down the slope.

"What is it?"

"I saw something."

Aundrém scanned the walls with his torchlight. Nothing moved save shadow. After a moment Gaijori sheathed his sword and they resumed their descent.

After what felt like an endless plunge through darkness, the floor levelled off. Ahead, a pale, cold glow lit the walls with frosty highlights. Their torches guttered and were gone at a gesture from Aundrém. Cautiously, they stepped towards the glow, drawing their swords.

The tunnel disgorged into a huge cavern, so vast the roof and walls were lost in gloom. A ruin sprawled across the cavern floor, witch-lights hanging from its nitred walls and nestling in corners, bathing the crumbled remains in a blue-white glow. Gaijori stepped forward, lost in awe.

It was incredibly old, so much was plain. The narrow streets were paved with crushed stone and mortar from the tall, erratic buildings leaning drunkenly above them. Fossilized wooden shutters hung from disintegrating hinges. Deep, wide trenches – ancient canals, perhaps – ran tortuous paths throughout the city, the remains of what Gaijori guessed to be bridges fallen across them. The cavern itself might once have been below the sea: clumps of dead coral and smashed shells littered the floor, fish skeletons were embedded in the walls.

They scrambled down into one dry canal, climbing the ruin of a shattered bridge to a narrow, winding alley. Reaching a dead end they chose a right-hand turn onto another street. They moved through twisting, dimly-lit streets, swords always ready. Aundrém also drew one of his wheellocks. Shadowy things backed into cover as they passed, clattering on spindly legs or wriggling silently.

Aundrém's shout was timely. Gaijori looked up to see a number of creatures dropping towards them on threads which shimmered as though coated by an oily film. Part squid, part scorpion, they wriggled awkwardly on armoured tentacles. Each had several articulated stingers raised to strike.

Aundrém fired a pistol directly into one of the things. It twitched, leaking dark blood, but refused to die. Swords flashed in the half-light, hacking at the armoured flesh. Gaijori's sword moaned softly; Aundrém's black blade seemed to radiate its own shadows. Together they wrought terrible damage, but the things seemed indifferent to harm. Squirming across the ground as long as there was a limb to drag them, lashing with their stingers. They spat oily threads.

Aundrém and Gaijori stood back to back, facing the oncoming creatures, almost as they had back in the Graav's garden. In a short time, butchered yet still moving corpses filled the street. Eventually the survivors backed away, turning their attentions to easier prey, hauling chunks of twitching remains into the darkness.

Gaijori pulled off his helm, letting it dangle absently. He rubbed a shaking hand across his face. "Is this hell?" he muttered, voice trembling with reaction.

Aundrém drew his second pistol, shrugging the now empty pommel holster off his shoulder. "Very likely." Tucking the wheellock through his sword belt he carefully stepped over carcasses. More than one snapped at his ankles. Gaijori wondered if Aundrém knew where he was going, or if he was simply acting on a whim.

They moved through the streets, turning left and right in what felt like random choices. They crossed a small, white bridge. Below, filling the canal, writhed a solid greasy mass. Snakes, Gaijori wondered. Some composite organism? He chose not to dwell on the thought.

Eventually, they emerged from a narrow alley into a wide plaza. A familiar, rainbow-flecked radiance hung above it, filling the square with dancing light. Gaijori's skin reflected the kaleidoscopic pulses of colour, his tattoos seemed to throb with a life of their own.

To their right marched colonnades. A tall, red-bricked tower reached for the roof, disappearing into the darkness beyond the hovering glow. On their left was a once magnificent palace, roofed with gilt domes and surrounded by a loggia which still bore traces of purple and red paint. Beyond the plaza was impenetrable blackness. Outlined against it stood a tall, fluted column, mounted by what Gaijori thought was a winged statue. Until it moved.

"Hold!" echoed a cracked voice. "Declare thy natures to me!"

It raised what looked like an old bulky musket, aiming at the two men. It was in many ways similar to the dead Qrymh, except this creature's faceted eyes blazed a deep, feverish blue, and it had four stout legs and two misshapen arms. Wings sprouted from its back. A faint, pearly glow engulfed it.

"This is the other sorcerer?" said Gaijori. "Qryvi?"

"A wretched shell, I think, with little of her powers left. The Qryvi I knew had no taste for firearms." Aundrém's face was drawn and pinched. He looked uncertain.

The creature waved its long musket. "We hear thy speech, black one!" The voice trembled with fear, or madness. "Tell us thy nature!"

"It's I, Qryvi: Annwyl," replied Aundrém. He raised his basket-hilted sword.

Qryvi leaned forward, peering down intently, compound eyes alight. "Annwyl the Raven? Yet thou hast changed not at all, while we—" The hoarse voice choked off. After a moment, Qryvi straightened and turned her blue eyes on Gaijori. "Thou dost bear the look of one of ours. Have they sent thee? Dost thou have the blood of our dearest brother on thy hands?"

"He is not Qrymh's killer—" began Aundrém.

Qryvi's voice rose above his, drowning it. "We did not ask thee, sweet-lipped Raven! Scion of one twice dead! Thy promises may be centuries old, but we hear them afresh each day. Hold thy tongue!" Her faceted eyes glared down on Gaijori.

Anything to take his gaze away, he bowed low. "Lady Qryvi, I am but lately come to this land. The one known to you as Annwyl and I chanced upon the body of your brother, the Lord Qrymh. He did not die by my hand, nor by that of my companion. Neither of us have the means nor the motive."

"Very courtly," whispered Aundrém.

"Then thou dost underestimate thy companion, my child." The glowing eyes dimmed and turned away. "As did we all." Qryvi glanced at the radiance hanging over the plaza. "But thou, at least, doth speak true. That which crushed our brother's heart is beyond thee. Beyond us all..."

She looked down at Gaijori again. The anger was gone from the inhuman eyes, the tremor from her voice. "Approach us, my son. Tell us thy name." She was gentle, cajoling.

He bowed again but moved no closer. "I am Gaijori Akkanëyodi, Lady Qryvi, lately from the shores of Vainë-kyuni. Perhaps you have heard of it?"

She laughed, a sad sound which echoed around the plaza. "Ah, my child, we know it well. We knew it as both paradise and hell. Approach, and tell us thou dost forgive us."

Gaijori glanced at Aundrém. "What does she mean?"

The other stared at the slabs under his feet. He seemed reluctant to speak. "Qrymh, Qryvi and their seven brothers and sisters ruled a land to the west. They created life to populate that land, including beings in their own image."

Gaijori's stomach did a slow turn.

"However, they quarrelled." Aundrém's voice was distant, thoughts clearly far away. "Annwyl tried to stop them – *I* tried to stop them. I knew what would happen if they indulged in civil war."

"And when reason failed, black-sword did play the suitor." From above some of the anger had returned to Qryvi's tone and eyes. "He seduced us before fleeing. He deserted us."

"No!" Aundrém raised his head. "You know I tried to save you, get you clear of your brother's influence. But you were just as headstrong. So convinced you were in the right! I could not stay once war had begun—"

"You're talking about Vainë-kyuni," Gaijori murmured. He did not mean it as a question.

Aundrém sighed. "The war inevitably left their paradise broken. Land twisted, sky in perpetual torment. Much of the life was subtly altered, none more so than the nine themselves. They fled to other Tiers – in shame, perhaps. I know where the seven resettled, but Qrymh and Qryvi successfully hid themselves away."

Gaijori began to shiver. He pointed his crimson sword at Qryvi. "*That* created Vainë-kyuni? That miserable, insane ... *monster!*" His helm slipped from his grasp.

Qryvi reared, faceted eyes once more burning with cold blue fury, wings outstretched. She raised the musket. "Silence! Bow thy knee to us! Prostrate thyself! Pray to thy god!"

Gaijori snatched the pistol from Aundrém's belt. His inexpert shot hit Qryvi's right shoulder. She gasped and clutched at the wound, dropping the musket. It fell to the paved square, gunpowder exploding harmlessly.

"This is a madhouse!" Gaijori's voice was all but drowned by echoes.

"Madhouse indeed."

The voice was soft but still audible above the bedlam. Gaijori and Aundrém spun about, swords coming on guard.

A tall, gaunt man stepped from the palace's shadowed arches. Like Aundrém he was all in black, but of a style unfamiliar to Gaijori. His jerkin seemed to be spun from some kind of web, his high-topped boots tanned from a scaly hide. A heavy cloak draped his frame, his gloved left hand resting on the hilt of a large sword. His green eyes were pools of deep misery.

Aundrém swore. The point of his sword wavered uncertainly. "I thought you just a story!" he muttered.

A pained look passed fleetingly through the stranger's eyes. "I know you." His voice was deep, steady. "Raven. Though that is but one of many names. Many lives..."

"You're the Voidal." Aundrém spoke the name as though it was poison.

"*Voidal!*" Qryvi's cry reawakened the echoes, her wound forgotten.

"Our brother's killer! Annwyl, if ever thou didst love us, destroy it!"

The gaunt man looked up at the trembling figure, frowning, puzzlement in his eyes. His left hand rubbed at his forehead. "You seem to know me too, but I don't... Ah – the dreams!" He groaned softly before falling silent again.

"'Twas that damned golden sword, Krysolac!" Qryvi's faceted eyes stared into the shadows beyond the square. "He gifted us with it, telling us we might use it to flee the Boundless. That we could start afresh! He led us to the Wild Precincts where even Infinity ends. We did hurl it at the Interface."

"And ruptured it briefly." Aundrém's eyes flickered to the Voidal and back. "Who gave you Krysolac?"

"The Shapeless One!" Qryvi was growing ever more agitated, her many limbs restless, her wings snapping. Gaijori thought she might fall at any moment.

"Shilnoth? You'd believe a creature whose lies outnumber his infinite lips over me?" Aundrém's laugh was bitter. "Where is Krysolac now?"

"Lost! We were hurled uncontrollably back through the Tiers. The sword is gone."

"I recall a dream," murmured the Voidal. "Or a dream of a dream. A great golden sword. A bargain; a threat. Ah, it fades—"

The Dark Man's voice reminded Qryvi of his presence "Begone, Voidal! Thou dost not belong here! Begone – lest I destroy thee!"

Gaijori thought he saw some multi-limbed thing wriggle around the fluted column. It vanished too quickly for him to be certain.

"Begone? To where?" The Voidal sounded genuinely puzzled. "I have no intention of harming you."

"Not hurt me? Yet Qrymh is dead—" she gestured at the radiance hovering overhead "—and thou art he who killed him!"

The Voidal stiffened, as at a sudden pain. Freeing his right arm from his cloak he stared at the handless wrist.

Qryvi cried out in alarm. A dark shape, as large and many limbed as she, rose over the top of the column. Although bathed in the flickering light above the plaza it had no more depth than a shadow. It latched onto Qryvi, black limbs wrapping themselves around her. She tried to fight back, but the shape expanded, slowly engulfing her, breaking wings, crushing arms and legs. Qryvi wailed in despair as her head was consumed by the shadow. A moment later a black tangle rolled off the column and smashed onto the slabs.

Aundrém ran to the foot of the column. Gaijori followed him, warily. The opalescence which had surrounded Qryvi was already shrinking, withdrawing into a glowing cloud over her body. There was no sign of the thing which had killed her.

Aundrém sheathed his sword and knelt beside the crushed body. Tenderly, he laid a hand on the inhuman face. "I did love thee, Qryvi," he whispered, barely loud enough for Gaijori to hear. "Rest now."

The shimmering cloud drifted higher, mixing with all that remained of her brother. For a moment the conjoined essences pulsed with a single blinding light then, with a mournful sigh, they dissipated into the shadows. The plaza was left in semi-darkness, a mere handful of witch lights barely holding back the gloom.

Gaijori turned away from Qryvi's corpse. The one called the Voidal stood before him, holding out the Vainë-kyuni helm. As Gaijori took it, he noticed the man's right hand was once more in place. He shuddered.

"Let us leave," he muttered. He was tired and angry. He'd left Vainë-kyuni to satisfy his curiosity, now he wished he'd remained in ignorance. "I hope the horses are still there."

Aundrém shook his head. "It's been a pleasure to know you, friend Gaijori, though I'm sure you're close to hating me at this moment. Our paths separate here. You cannot come where I'm heading – even if you wished to."

Gaijori looked at both men in black. He thought he understood. "The Voidal—?"

"Does not belong here. I must try to return him to his own reality; his own dark, sealed corner of the Boundless." He smiled: a pained facsimile of his usual cocky grin. "And there is the small matter of a lost sword."

"You're a romantic." Gaijori tried not to make it sound like an accusation.

"We both are, I think. A pity the Internection has little regard for such as we."

Gaijori tried to smile back, but he did not have Aundrém's resilience. Or was it cynicism. He turned and strode away.

"Remember what I said regarding the Swords," Aundrém called after him. "Or do you think it was just bleak irony that I was the one who witnessed Qryvi's final moments? A reminder that even Eternals may die."

Gaijori ignored him. As he ignored the eyes he sensed watching him leave: from men dressed all in black, and from the haunted ruin through which he would once more have to pass.

His hand caressed Sangrinn's hilt.

THE AIRS OF EDEN

RHYMA BOWED OVER her flowerbed, waiting for the one standing nervously behind her to speak.

"My lady?"

She straightened, turning slowly, feigning surprise, as though she hadn't known Issuk had been there all this time. She looked down over her imposing aquiline nose; she knew it made her look stern. His deceptively innocent face was set in an uncertain smile.

"What is it?"

He glanced at the ground, turned his head briefly as though expecting to see someone coming through the rows of vines stretching into the misty distance, then looked back up at her. "I saw a stranger, my lady."

"A stranger?" Rhyma stood taller, leaning on a plain wooden staff that was almost her height, and gave Issuk a smile of her own. He had been out in the orchards, collecting ripened fruit with his friends. Was he about to blame the handfuls he had eaten on some fanciful stranger – despite the purple evidence staining his teeth and corners of his mouth? "And what did this stranger look like? All in black, perhaps?"

It was not unknown for a passing Inquisitor to occasionally help themselves to some of Erberow's ever-present harvest, much as it irked Rhyma – not that even she would ever dare protest. And that wily rascal Marudwy – or whatever alias he was presently hiding behind – was a frequent pilferer. But she always knew when they were near, and she had not felt any of their presences recently. Nor any other.

Issuk was shaking his head. "No, my lady. It was in armour, I think. Colourful, it was. Glittering like a dragonfly."

Rhyma's smile evaporated. She dropped to one knee to look Issuk directly in the eyes. "Tell me truthfully now, was this stranger about my height, yet look stooped? Its armour hanging down from the shoulders, more like a cloak? And did it wear a helm, a strangely shaped one, with large eye slits, black, with nothing to see behind them?"

Issuk looked alarmed. "It seemed to be formed into an ugly face. Scary."

Rhyma ruffled his black hair. "Get back to the orchards. Tell everyone they may stop for the day. Collect everything you've picked and take it to the barns, then go and play."

Issuk nodded, still uncertain. Rhyma grinned at him. "Or would you rather tell me about all those cyla berries you've been eating?"

He stepped away, expression suddenly shy. "I'll tell everyone, my lady." He turned and hurried back in the direction of the vineyard.

Rhyma levered herself upright, leaning heavily on her staff. Despite a mane of hair that was now more grey than red, and an increasing number of wrinkles appearing on her face, she did not consider herself old. She was an Eternal: immortal, timeless. Such as her did not grow old.

"Tell that to my knees," she muttered softly.

Slowly she scanned the landscape stretching away in all directions. The vineyard, orchards to her left and right, gardens blooming with countless flowers and their attendant pollinators gathered from every level of the Infinite Tiers: woodland, forest and jungle. And much, much more. Erberow did not occupy infinite space – not quite – but it was a Tier unto itself. An almost endless world upon which life in all its infinite variety flourished, providing food, drink and a haven to all the dispossessed and lost souls who Rhyma had gathered and nurtured. Those rejected by their own worlds, now able to live out their mayfly existences in safety and comfort.

She shrugged. Erberow was hardly a paradise: things died here just as readily as on any mortal plane. But there was, she hoped, no cruelty. No suffering.

But now this stranger that Issuk had seen. In armour, wearing a helm shaped like a face. One who had entered Erberow completely unknown to Rhyma. Not even an Inquisitor, with all their chilly cunning, could manage that, and it troubled her. It troubled her deeply.

With a heavy sigh she headed towards the left-hand orchard. Issuk and his friends had been harvesting there. With luck the newcomer would still be in the vicinity.

Rhyma snorted. *Luck! With real luck they would be gone, never to be seen again!*

She travelled quickly, her tall staff striking the ground with a hollow thud at each step, covering the distance with a speed that would alarm Issuk and his friends. Well, she was in a hurry – although far from eager.

She located the newcomer easily enough, almost as though it wanted to be found. Wandering among the twisted boughs of cyla bushes, brushing a hand encased in what may have been a gauntlet across the red leaves and clustered berries. At least it wasn't eating them.

The figure paused and looked up at Rhyma's approach. As she'd feared, what Issuk had thought a helm was in fact the creature's head: encased in a hard chitinous material, with large black compound eyes and several jutting antennae growing from the crown. They moved slowly, two swivelling in Rhyma's direction. Something like a cloak draped its slouched body, fashioned from hardened leather – or perhaps the same chitinous material as its head. Its limbs were hidden.

It slouched lower as she neared: a crude bow. A harsh, stridulant voice came from the head as the lower half split into jointed mouthparts. "Duchess Ellyn of Erberow."

"I have not used that title since the Internection was but two fledgling universes contemplating a family. I am Rhyma – no more, no less. State your business here." Although she feared she already knew.

A strident hiss escaped the thing's head as its many mandibles opened and shut. Rhyma had the distinct impression it was laughing at her.

"We seek supplies, your grace. Erberow is large, rich and fertile – it can spare us enough for our needs."

"And who is 'we', might I ask?"

"Travellers between the Tiers. We find ourselves bereft of nourishment, and we throw ourselves on your grace's mercy – which we understand is legendary."

"Travellers, is it?" Rhyma took her staff in both hands. "I think ravagers would be a more apt description. You are from a Zzyschyth Swarm, are you not? And what will you do if I refuse your request?"

The thing hissed again. "I think you know the answer to that."

Rhyma levelled her staff, aiming one tip directly at the creature. "Don't think it will be so easy..."

"You are ancient, your grace—"

"Thanks for reminding me."

"—while we are many."

"Erberow is not without defences."

The Zzyschyth's insect-like head shook, its mandibles working. "A few mortals? And of those so many no more than youngsters. They cannot prevail."

"They may not have to."

Rhyma struck without warning, her staff a blur of motion. The

Zzyschyth leapt nimbly away, its movements staccato. The cloak draping its form rose, splitting into sections like a beetle's carapace. Underneath, its body was gaunt and even more insectile. It poised itself on two thin legs, while four more limbs clutched a variety of ugly weapons. Hooked, with toothed blades, they were clearly designed more for reaping than fighting, scything down anything within reach and reducing it to the smallest morsels. Rhyma gazed at the creature with contempt, imagining the suffering such tools would force on their victims.

"I abhor violence," she said quietly. "Too often it merely breeds more destruction. But in your case, butcher bug, I think I will make an exception. Perhaps I should return you to your kin in mouthful delicacies."

The Zzyschyth hissed a laugh and raised all four arms. It spread its carapace and shook the weapons in what it likely hoped was an intimidating manner. Rhyma's answer was to spin her staff, dance closer, and crack its tip against the creature's spindly body.

Caught off balance it half-stumbled, using its many limbs to regain its equilibrium. Rhyma used its momentary distraction to come in closer still, striking it across the head, the carapace; driving her staff's tip between the flailing limbs and deep into the gaunt thorax. She felt something crack under the impact.

Rhyma retreated several paces. The Zzyschyth regained its feet, coming upright. She was sure she saw hatred in its compound eyes.

Good. Let it hate her; let it grow reckless with fury.

Wings unfurled from beneath its carapace. It came at her, leaping high in the air and pouncing, the butcher weapons in all four arms striking at her head and shoulders. Rhyma evaded them easily, swinging her staff hard at the skeletal limbs.

One snapped. The Zzyschyth's lower left arm folded in two, nearly coming apart. The scything weapon clutched in its narrow fingers fell to the ground. The creature danced away again, keening like a boiling kettle.

Rhyma grounded her staff. She almost felt sorry for the thing. She knew this was the moment to strike, to finish it. But she was reluctant. Even one as miserable as this had a right to its own existence.

It stared back at her, shattered left limb cradled by the lower right one. It stooped even more.

"Go," said Rhyma. "Leave Erberow. I have no wish to destroy you, but I will if I must."

"You cannot defeat us all!" Its sibilant voice was strained and harsh. "We will engulf your sweet vines and orchards. We will feast. We will leave nothing in our wake!"

"Return and you will die. All of you. I have no wish for it – but I will eradicate your swarm if I must."

"You overestimate yourself, your grace. Enjoy this paradise while you may. When next we meet I will enjoy discovering how swiftly an Eternal dies..."

The Zzyschyth stepped back, its carapace and wings spreading wider. For a moment it seemed to Rhyma that the Zzyschyth's body turned sideways, becoming flat, like an image painted onto paper or canvas, then it vanished. Slipping into the air, returning to whatever devastated realm its swarm presently inhabited.

Rhyma sighed, leaning heavily upon her staff. She needed to gather

Issuk and his friends together – all of the mortals presently working or playing in this part of the garden. They could not hope to survive what that thing would lead here. They must leave, and quickly.

❦ ❦ ❦

SHE STOOD ON a short rocky outcrop, one of many growing incrementally taller to join with the towering cliff face at her back. Vegetation was spare here: mosses and lichens sprouting from cracks in the boulders or spreading themselves tenuously over their faces. A few alpine plants hung on gamely, but this was a cold and infertile corner of Erberow, and life teetered on the edge. It was not a place where the coming swarm would find much to enjoy.

Her crude dais was clustered about by a crowd of restless, anxious mortals. Issuk and his many friends, other young ones from the many groups who were spread throughout Rhyma's gardens. And there were older mortals too, ones who had been as young as Issuk once, but whose brief lives had brought them to maturity in less time than a blink. They would die soon, just as Issuk and his friends would become adults, and inevitably pass on. Generations upon generations, more than Rhyma cared to consider. Some being born to Erberow, knowing no other life, many more plucked from a heart-breaking existence and allowed to continue their lives among the flowers and vines. Mortal lives were too short to register much on the infinite breadth and existence of the Boundless, but fleeting as those lives were, Rhyma did not like any to be cut shorter than necessary.

Most of the upturned faces were creased in sorrow, some wet with tears. Others, especially among the youngest, were blank with incomprehension. Issuk's expression was typically stubborn.

"We don't want to!" he said, for the third time.

"Believe me, I wish you didn't have to," sighed Rhyma. "But what is coming will have no more respect for you than you do for a gnat. If they acknowledge you at all, it will be as an irritant – and they will likely consume you as eagerly as anything else in my gardens."

Several of the really young began to wail at that. Rhyma was regretful, but if terror gave them more urgency, well—

"But where shall we go?" asked one of the grown ones. Tokreth was his name – or so Rhyma thought. It was so hard to recognise their faces as they aged.

"Somewhere safe. A place where not even an Inquisitor could find you. Or not easily, at least."

"How?" persisted Tokreth.

"A way that you have gone before." But have since forgotten, she added silently.

She raised her staff, holding it horizontal. A cunning twist of one tip, and it slid back, revealing a small hole. A mouthpiece. Rhyma placed it to her lips, the staff now a long, clumsy flute. She began to play a low, mournful tune, summoning it from the instrument without holes, just subtleties in her breathing. There were as many types of Erberowan wind-pipe as there were sizes and ways to play them, but all had one thing in common: their effect on the mortal mind and reality. A merry jig would have an entire city dancing in moments, a lament bringing the same people to tears just as quickly. The fiercest heart could be tamed, the most stubborn mind made to accept, the most timid fired to the greatest acts of courage. And they could lead whole populations from their hovels and through the strangest thresholds they would ever have seen, into a better, kinder world.

As Rhyma played, Erberow fell still. The creatures of the air quieted their squeaks and shrieks, the tiny beasts foraging in the nooks and cracks in the rock stopped and listened. Even the wind fell away. The crowd surrounding Rhyma's perch became silent, watching her intently, their eyes already focusing on something far beyond Erberow, their faces filled with rapture.

She blew a sudden high trill – a descant over the low melody – fluttering a hand in the air, careful not to drop her large flute. Behind her she heard the grind of shifting rocks, the sounds of dirt and tiny pebbles cascading from a disturbed cliff face. Coaxing a final tuneful flourish from her instrument, she lowered it, turning to look at the cliff.

A high chasm had split the rocks, three times higher than the tallest in the crowd and wide enough to take three abreast. It was dark and shadowed, but a faint, encouraging glow came from somewhere deep inside.

Rhyma took a steadying breath. It consumed most of her strength and all of her will playing such a tune, opening a way through to another Tier. A sub-Tier in fact, created from crude matter then populated with everything these mortals would need, no matter how long the stay. She hadn't attempted such a thing since she had raised Erberow up from nothing, and the Boundless had been young back then. As she had been.

She twisted her flute and closed the end, once more returning it to a staff configuration. She placed one tip at her feet and leaned on it, trying hard not to show how spent she was.

"Quickly now – go though. I will call you back when it's safe."

As one the crowd looked from her to the rift in the cliff face, their expressions no less rapturous. Carefully they climbed over the rocks and boulders, never taking their eyes from the gap and the distant glow. As Rhyma watched, they filed into the chasm and vanished into the darkness.

Once the last had disappeared into the chasm Rhyma allowed herself to sag. She sat down on the rocky outcrop, trying to ignore the stiffness in every joint. She was almost the same age as the Internection, and if she was starting to suffer from all those thousands of millennia, was the Boundless also ageing? It wasn't a cheerful thought.

She was shaken from her thoughts by another rumble. The cleft in the rock face was closing, healing from the top downwards. Soon there was no indication there had ever been any form of gap. No scar, not even the smallest crack.

Rhyma pulled herself to her feet. She was still tired, drained from playing her flute, but there were things to do, things to consult.

She began to walk down from the cool rocky heights.

ERBEROW HELD MANY different dwellings, from the lowliest to the most palatial. Rhyma had long ago noticed curious behaviours among the mortals she had rescued: at first they would settle into the most luxurious palaces but, after a while, they would often leave and find themselves a home closer to the ones they had known in their earlier lives. More comfortable, perhaps, simpler. And often with others of their kind, in a type of family collective. Being in familial groups seemed to make them more comfortable. Rhyma had existed almost since time began, but had never felt the urge for a family. Few Eternals did. Her hordes of rescued mortals didn't count.

Her own home stood deep within a section of forest that had been allowed to run wild. A tangle of walls, towers and buttresses, it looked as natural as the many gnarled trees clustered about it, as though it, too, had slowly grown from a seed, becoming wizened with age.

She walked through a drooping doorway, throwing her staff carelessly among a tangle of rootlets curling out of an arched wall, and made her way deeper into the chaotic dwelling. It was a spacious construction, as large as many of the palaces she had created, but with no obvious internal logic. Many young mortals, urged on by the curiosity which seemed endemic in the species, had entered while she was absent and become hopelessly lost, only to be freed once she returned and felt their presence and terror.

She wished she could sense the arrival of the coming swarm as easily.

Rhyma entered a chamber where she kept her few items of clothing. It was spherical, networked throughout by gnarled roots or branches, all of which were shot through with veins of flickering light in bright greens and reds. Walking directly from one side to another was impossible. She preferred it that way.

At the far end of the strange chamber, various items of clothing hung from branchlike shapes twisting from the uneven wall. With an unexpected pang of nostalgia, Rhyma reached for one lengthy garment which seemed to have been patched together from a hundred contrasting suits, in every colour and shade. It was ragged and shapeless, and when shrugged on it dragged on the floor in several places. When she moved it rustled like a soft breeze through the trees. On another twig dangled a disreputable feathered beret, just as motley. Rhyma placed it on her head, tilting it so one side drooped past her right ear at a rakish angle, and tucked underneath as much of her greying hair as she could.

A section of wall to her left was polished to a mirror surface. She took a moment to admire herself and her fluttering robe. Then she took another flute down from where it hung above the mirror – smaller than her staff, with several slots cut into its black surface – and began to wave it.

She moved the flute in complex arabesques – whirling it above her head and around her body – rolling the instrument as she did so. No sound came from the flute, but she heard it nonetheless: a melody played beyond Erberow, sweet and clear, flowing like a river after the spring rains. The dancing flute summoned and conducted it, sending the melody spiralling through the Infinite Tiers, searching, probing.

And as the unheard music played, the polished section before Rhyma began to expand. Slowly it grew, spreading gradually across the whole uneven wall, replacing it with a warped mirror that partly reflected the chamber, partly itself. Endless images of the chamber plunged deep into the surface, disappearing only when they became too small to be clearly seen.

Rhyma slowed her flute's motion, gradually bringing it to a stop.

The unheard melody died – but the warped mirror and its twisted reflections remained. Rhyma placed the flute on the uneven floor, since the hook from which it had hung was no longer there – absorbed into the mirror – and stared critically at her creation.

It was an imperfect model of the Boundless since, despite the apparent infinity of self-reflected images, it was bounded by finite space. It would do, though. She might not be able to sense where the Zzyschyth Swarm would break through into Erberow, but her virtual image of the Internection should track its progress through the Tiers. The tune her flute had created still played throughout the infinite realms and Tiers and would play all the louder wherever it found the Swarm. Like an echo bouncing back from a deep, dark ravine.

All she had to do now was wait – and that came easily to one whose concept of time was far less linear than that of the mortals she tended.

❦ ❦ ❦

A **BRIEF SNATCH** of melody alerted her. Rhyma leaned forward, squinting as she stared hard at the reflected chamber and its regression of images before her. More of the echoed melody played back.

There was nothing to see in the mirrored wall, nonetheless Rhyma located the Zzyschyth Swarm. It was massing close to an underpopulated area of Erberow, ready to transition and begin its assault.

Rhyma turned and reached past a tangle of veined roots. Her hand closed over a narrow shaft. It came free, and in her hand was a tall staff not unlike her original one, save it seemed to be made from something like polished dark wood or metal, yet neither, and weighed almost nothing. Its tips were sheathed in a shimmering golden material. An irregular network of coarse ridges ran from tip to tip, covering the shaft.

Facing the mirror wall again, Rhyma took a deep breath. Then she raised the dark staff and thrust one end directly into the reflective surface. There was the sound of shattering crystal. The wall and its endless images flew apart—

—and Rhyma found herself standing under a dim sun, surrounded by a dank, dark jungle. Thick black trunks and twisted branches dripped with sodden moss. The ground underfoot squelched. In moments her scuffed shoes were soaked. There wasn't a sound aside from the irregular trickle of water. Overhead, steely clouds roiled.

The Swarm had chosen an ideal place to come through. With no witnesses they could be halfway across Erberow, stripping it bare, before they expected Rhyma to be alerted.

She trudged through cold mud, seeking higher ground and a vantage point. The Swarm might appear at any moment.

The terrain sloped upward. The black trees thinned out, giving way to drier, harder ground that still had an oily film of mud across it. Rhyma slipped more than once as the incline increased.

Eventually she reached the peak: a narrow, rocky crag far above the dank jungle. Rhyma could see clearly in all directions. A cold wind snatched at her ragged clothing, plucked at her feathered beret.

Again she waited.

The clouds split, spinning open to reveal a black void against which countless gaunt shapes twitched and shifted. A moment later, the Zzyschyth Swarm slipped through into Erberow: a dark numberless horde drifting towards the ground. Their massed chirps and hisses was almost like a roar of defiance.

Rhyma raised her staff. She had regained much of her strength during her wait, but she was still weary. She sucked in a breath of chilly air, willing her vitality to return.

The Swarm's vanguard approached, settling on the thick jungle, already hacking at the dripping boughs with their scythe-like weapons. They would get little nourishment there, Rhyma thought. Even so, the full Swarm would reduce the black trees to stumps in no time.

A smaller group of six Zzyschyth broke off from the vanguard, gliding straight towards her. Rhyma was not surprised to see one had a shattered forelimb – crudely bound together and immobilised against the creature's thorax.

"Come to lose the rest of your limbs?" she called, her voice almost drowned beneath the Swarm's chittering.

The injured Zzyschyth howled something incomprehensible and landed on the crag less than a stone's throw from Rhyma. "Enjoy your last taunt, your grace! Now we are legion!"

The creature bounded forward, three of its forelimbs wielding cruel toothed weapons. Rhyma's fingers danced along the shaft of her dark staff. Long, curved blades – as hooked and barbed as the Zzyschyth's own – flicked out of the gilded tips. She swung the staff. The Zzyschyth was unable to slow its charge. A moment later its chitinous body fell to the cold ground, bisected. Green blood pooled around the remains.

"And now you are one less," murmured Rhyma.

The rest of the group pounced, certain of victory. Rhyma spun her bladed staff, blocking their overconfident attack easily. The Zzyschyth fell back, blood oozing from cuts to their abdomens and thoraxes. One limped heavily, suffering a serious injury to a skeletal leg. Rhyma advanced down from the crag, pressing her assault. The five Zzyschyth retreated further, becoming four as the seriously injured one was cut down by the blades of Rhyma's whirling staff.

As it moved, the staff crooned a mournful tune, played by the passage of air across its ridged surface. A soft lilt, barely discernible above the Swarm.

The four Zzyschyth regrouped, trying to surround Rhyma, but she spun and pivoted gracefully, the blurred arc of her staff seeming to be everywhere. One by one the Zzyschyth were cut down. Their green blood mingled with the muddy ground, making it ever more slippery.

The Swarm continued to descend from the cold air. Black trees were hewn apart, and articulated mouthparts fastened on the felled timber, chewing noisily. Sodden moss was sucked down piecemeal. Gnawing sounds grew in volume, slowly drowning out the endless chittering.

Rhyma surveyed the growing carnage. Something like fury possessed her, burning past her weariness, igniting fresh vigour. She charged down into the jungle and the feasting Swarm, her staff spinning, the two blades reaping a harvest of their own.

Generally, the Zzyschyth ignored her. A few fought back or tried to halt her advance, but she was mostly disregarded. She was but one; they existed in hundreds of thousands. No matter how many she destroyed, it would be but a fraction of the Swarm. And once they had taken as much as they could from the matted jungle, they would be gone – skimming away to another part of Erberow, likely one less barren. The Zzyschyth were a pragmatic species, willing to sacrifice a few so that the majority might go on.

Congealing green blood coated her staff from tip to tip and its dirge grew louder, almost gleeful, as though fed by the gore. The tune played across the decimated woodland, carried on the cold air. It spread further. It grew loud enough for the Swarm to hear above their own clamour. A few paused, uncertain, looking about the cloudy skies as though wondering what the mournful tune meant.

Rhyma pressed on, destroying individuals even as the Swarm reduced the wet jungle to stumps and shreds. Her fury had abated somewhat, leaving her tired, tormented with self-hatred at her actions. Life was life, after all; but a gardener will always do what is necessary to protect the garden. She had to be as practical as the Zzyschyth.

Her staff now sang with a voice loud enough to drown out the Swarm. It was a cry of outrage, of pain. A distillation of all the self-loathing filling Rhyma's breast. It was a cry for help.

Many more of the Zzyschyth paused, looking up from their half-devoured roosts. Concern etched their strange features, doubt hunched their gaunt bodies. The antennae on their heads twitched nervously.

Rhyma lowered her staff, although its lament still echoed across the bleak landscape. Now that she had the Swarm's attention, it was possible it would attack her out of fear and panic. Not that it would do them much good.

"You misunderstand the nature of Erberow!" she called. Her staff wove an eerie harmony around her voice, amplifying it. "It is not just a vast, fruitful garden and home for rejected mortals – *all* are welcome. Any dispossessed soul from any corner of the Infinite Tiers, no matter what their nature, save that they are lost in some way. Creatures that are not so weak and helpless. Beings from realms that are as far removed from my orchards as this mud is from the stars – realms that are recreated in Erberow. To them, in your own words, they are a paradise. And they are vengeful creatures who will do what they can to ensure they do not lose that paradise again."

Dozens of Zzyschyth reared up from their decimated tree stumps. Their compound eyes were raised to the grey skies, antennae straining to sense the faintest disturbance.

"You bluff, ancient one!" buzzed a lone voice. Rhyma could not tell which of the Zzyschyth had spoken.

"Ancient I may be, plague-bug, but I am not, as you see, alone."

The skies were parting again. A dark, penetrating glow spread behind the clouds, boiling them away. From the vast glowing abyss poured more shapes: humanoid, fishlike, globular, fungoid. Forms that were not so easily described. All from the strangest and most distant shores of Erberow, swooping towards the cropped jungle and an alarmed Swarm.

Clouds of Zzyschyth rose into the air to confront the beings. They bared their butcher weapons, buzzing a strident challenge. Rhyma could see they were confident in their sheer numbers.

Both sides clashed overhead. The Zzyschyth slashed and hacked with their cruel weapons. They had little effect on the flesh of the creatures they struck. Things of dark vapour smoked apart and reassembled after a blade's passage; scythes shattered on the huge, thick scales of winged fish creatures; blobs of glowing blue jelly oozed carelessly over the weapons and engulfed helpless Zzyschyth, digesting their absorbed bodies.

Every Zzyschyth abandoned the jungle on which they had hoped to begin their rape of Erberow and flew up to join the fight. Confronted by a force which held little regard for their weapons and numbers, the Zzyschyth assault faltered.

On the muddy ground, Rhyma raised her staff, hoping she had the strength for what she had to do next – both physically and emotionally. She began to spin the staff in complex whirls above her head, drawing invisible patterns on the air. All the while the staff wailed and moaned, the layer of congealed green blood gradually disappearing. Absorbed.

The earth shook. Trees already weakened by the Zzyschyth assault fell or shed branches. Mud heaved. Above it all, the Swarm continued to retreat from a slowly advancing aerial armada. The sky darkened where they were attempting to create a way off Erberow.

Rhyma shook her head. She could not allow them to flee and plague another realm.

The ground below the stripped jungle opened. Oily mud and gnawed vegetation fell into a void. Deep below, in a twilit darkness, dim shapes moved. Vast treelike forms which clutched at smaller, faster shapes dodging through the thick tentacle-like branches. A grinding, tearing cacophony rose from the void, blending with the voice of Rhyma's staff to create a hellish symphony.

"Now!" yelled Rhyma.

The defending armada halted its advance, backing away. The Zzyschyth Swarm, suspended far above, its threshold to another realm not yet complete, milled uncertainly.

Then Rhyma's staff began to croon a high, sorrowful lilt, turning the noises from the void into a sad lullaby. It pulled at the hovering Swarm, luring it, dragging it. Individuals tried to resist, but as an entity the Swarm was trapped. Like a tornado composed of living bodies it spun into a funnel and was sucked into the void. The heaving mass was gone in moments, the last handful of Zzyschyth falling with shrieks of despair. Then the ground sealed itself over the void, masking the sight of all those ravaging creatures fleeing from predatory trees.

"Devour or be devoured," sighed Rhyma. "Fitting, I suppose."

With a careful tap on her staff's ridged shaft, she collapsed its long blades and bowed deep and long to Erberow's defenders, who still filled the skies. Then forcing herself upright she raised the staff to her lips and blew once across the complex ridges. A deep note filled the air, making Rhyma's head and ears ring. The beings circling above her stilled, then flowed back into the dark radiance beyond the clouds.

Rhyma bowed once more, even though most of the things would not see her. She was grateful to them – more than grateful – and wished to show it, regardless.

The sky became normal. The clouds closed in. Rhyma felt the bitter cold through her ragged clothing, her feet were numb. She was beyond exhausted. Even so she managed a weak smile. Well, she *was* ancient, after all.

Resting her staff across a shoulder she began the long, weary trek back through the ruined jungle to the cliff face where she had hidden her most vulnerable blooms. The jungle was destroyed – either by the Zzyschyth or its fall into the void – but she could remake it. When she wasn't quite so tired.

Life, and Erberow, would go on.

141

HAND OF GLORY

GAIN HE'S YOUNG, naïve. Again he finds himself flanked by two formidable allies: one in glowing black, one an old woman in motley. Again they restrain him as two creatures battle to the death: one a flickering, insubstantial being that in the way of dreams he can't quite see; the other a man with eyes the colour of the crimson gem upon his hand. A man he has sought long and far to find. His father.

—And now he has found him, he will lose him. Again.

—But this time there is a difference: there is another actor in the drama. Always just out of sight, always hidden. Slinking around the tableau: angry, immeasurably powerful, frustrated...

—The duellers fight on, oblivious; discharging magics rarely wielded

by anything lower than the most powerful gods. One must die; two may.

—His father unleashes a withering stream of crimson. The flickering being falters, fades, rallies. The two close: the world shatters in a final, lethal eruption—

❦ ❦ ❦

HE JERKED AWAKE from the dream, engulfed by both guilt and relief. Relief that it was only a dream; guilt that he was still alive to experience it. He opened his eyes, flopping back in his cot, chilled by icy sweat.

Scarcely a moment later, the first mental wave hit: silver-edged and soundless. It consumed him, filling his senses with motion and colour enough to make up for the silence. He drowned in a malevolent rainbow; iridescent shapes wrapped tendrils around his throat, dragging him down.

It passed as abruptly as it had come.

He sat up, gasping, scrubbing harshly at his scalp, hoping to scour the vision away. What, by every devious god of the Internection, had *that* been?

The second wave hit before he could think of an answer.

This time, the formless blobs of colour gave way to figures: crude, blotched stick-men, hopelessly inept representations of living beings. They surged at his face, poked stick-weapons in his eyes. They called him names: *Andrhym, Myrdan, Aundrém—*

His vision cleared. He was on the wooden floor, on hands and knees, sucking air into burning lungs, trying not to vomit. All he could think of were the names. Was he Andrhym? Or Myrdan? No,

Aundrém – Marudwy. No! No, no, *no*—!

The third wave was no less agonising. This time the crude stickmen were clearer, but their confused actions made no more sense to him. A titanic, three-faced statue hacked through endless, overlying worlds with a white-hot sword, as though they were nothing more than the living tapestries they resembled. Figures no less gigantic crossed blades with a multi-armed creature composed of light. Clothed reptiles swarmed across a sterile desert, becoming dragons which roared and died in humid forests, becoming a horde overwhelming a golden-armoured figure whose face was engraved across its broad cuirass. Flying machines skimmed a slate-black forest of sharp rock, dodging oily tendrils hanging from clouds which filled a bronze sky.

And still a voice muttered a litany of names, familiar and new. *Annwyl, Andrion des Échelon, Andy Rome, Anij-Dré.* He thought he recognised that voice.

"No!"

His eyes cleared again. He was huddled on the floor, arms clutching his knees. This time he had vomited. The sour smell brought him back to the present.

"I am Elatrynn…" He unclenched his body, feeling every muscle crack and protest. "I am Elatrynn…!"

He pulled himself back onto his bed, casting a glance at the still sleeping figure across the tiny room. How had the motionless figure remained oblivious, with all hell breaking out around them? He rubbed his eyes and sighed. Stupid question. His companion wouldn't have heard, or felt, a thing. It had all been for Elatrynn's own, personal delight.

"Well, my thanks to you, whoever you might be," he croaked. His voice shook, his throat was raw. "Might I suggest a simple stone at the window or blade to the throat next time?"

Nevertheless, he felt a grudging respect for whoever had so rudely awoken him. To reach across the Infinite Tiers must necessarily require a vast amount of skill and power. If only they'd used it like a scalpel, and not a bludgeon.

He dressed. Loose blouse, trousers, leather jerkin and tall boots, all in black. Or had been once. His boots were scuffed and in dire need of polish, whilst the seams of his blouse were grey with wear. He rubbed at a beard that was in sore need of a trim. Crossing the darkened attic, gnarled floorboards protesting each step, he kicked at the other bed's nearest leg.

A half-concealed figure groaned and shifted in the cot. Green eyes peered from under a sheet, slipping into focus. A look of torment, familiar as old shoes, glazed them.

"Raven. So this dream, at least, is real?"

"As real as anything, my friend. Although that might be about to change."

The Voidal threw back his bedsheet and stood. He was already fully dressed, his clothing beyond black. "You know this how?"

Elatrynn reached under the cot and pulled out two swords. A large broadsword he handed to the Voidal, who took it with a look of distaste. An elaborately hilted black rapier he buckled around his own waist. "Just now, someone did their best to turn me into a drooling idiot with a sending. Someone who knows much about me." He slid the rapier a finger's length from its sheath and ran his thumb across the edge. "Too much."

"And this intrigues you?" The Voidal buckled on his large sword.

Elatrynn laughed. "Intrigues? The thought terrifies me more than you can imagine." He slammed his rapier back home. "And I will have answers."

"Beware of what you seek. It must come at a price."

Elatrynn thought of the Vainë-kyuni, Gaijori, and what he'd discovered of his own heritage. And he considered the legend of The Voidal: that for some crime against them, the strange gods who ruled a quarantine number of Tiers of the Boundless – somewhere beyond the Wild Precincts, according to poor, lost Qryvi – had filled him with ultimate knowledge, then stolen his memory. His identity. Only in dreams, and whenever they had a task for him, were scraps said to briefly return. Several times since leaving Qryvi's buried city, Elatrynn had almost asked the cursed man how much, if any, was true. On each occasion, one look into those green, tormented eyes had killed his curiosity.

Perhaps the two weren't so unalike. Elatrynn, with his ever-expanding catalogue of identities; the Voidal, with neither identity nor name. Both wanderers. That Elatrynn could normally choose his destination and alias made little difference. In the end both were rootless.

He shrugged off the mood. His rude awakening had made him melancholy. Stooping under his own cot he drew out a wide-brimmed black hat and jammed it on his head. It was as disreputable as the rest of his outfit. Elatrynn cocked it to a jaunty angle.

"Coming?" With a swagger, he crossed to the attic's only door and opened it. Beyond should have been narrow, rickety stairs.

Instead he was standing in a valley, its gentle slopes covered by a dark yellow grass. Under a lilac sky, low hills undulated to the horizon. Groves of black trunked, red-leafed trees dotted the landscape. A huge, bronze sun warmed the air, whilst an unfamiliar scent hung on the gentle breeze.

Elatrynn frowned. Ever since Qryvi's death he had been trying to make for the peripheral Tiers, even the Precincts themselves, in the hope that some way of returning the Voidal to his own realm might reveal itself. But with each transition the way grew more capricious. Once familiar waymarks moved or lost. This was the first time he had ever unconsciously moved between realms, however. It was not a novelty he enjoyed overmuch.

Elatrynn turned around, not at all surprised to see that the tumbled down inn with its cramped attic was no longer there. Nor was the lakeside town of Lidec, with its finicky inhabitants – for whom the Voidal's admittedly pallid skin was too light, while his own finely-tanned features were too dark. Just empty, yellow hills. And the Voidal, standing aloof and indifferent to the unheralded changes.

Elatrynn was not averse to the leaving of Lidec, but he considered the method left much to be desired.

On the brow of a hill, he noted the approach of six riders. His hand drifted to his sword hilt as they drew nearer. Their mounts were lithe, speckled creatures with long, multi-jointed limbs, and beaked heads from which grew huge tusks. The riders were encased in such brilliant, over-ornate armour it was impossible to tell their true shape.

They had already drawn weapons of an unfamiliar kind.

"A welcoming committee." Elatrynn drew his own sword. "How touching."

The Voidal folded his arms and watched the approaching riders as though they were nothing more than an intriguing form of wildlife.

The nearest rider pulled their mount to a halt. Their head, enclosed by a blue and gold helm fashioned into the most abstract shape, cocked to one side.

"You are not welcome!" The rider's voice was clear, despite the armour encasing their head. "I suggest you return from whence you came. Immediately!"

Elatrynn swept off his hat, made a leg and bowed deeply. "I would be pleased to oblige you, sir," he lied smoothly. "But, sadly, neither of us knows the way."

The rider raised a weapon resembling a cross between a sword and a sickle. "You would be advised not to jest with me: I have no remit to be gentle with vagabonds. The borders are sealed. I know not how you came here, but you will leave."

"Vagabond?" Elatrynn stood upright, his expression indignant.

"Are you not?" The Voidal's face was unreadable.

Elatrynn turned to face him. "Perhaps – technically ... but since we've yet to be formally acquainted, I think it's something of a presumption..."

"I lose patience!" the rider snapped. "Go back whence you came, or die here. Whichever is of supreme indifference to me."

Elatrynn's irritation returned. "*You're* losing patience! We have neither the intention nor the ability to return – especially as we don't know where the hell we are!"

"As you wish." The rider gestured languidly. "Kill them."

Five mounts sprang across the yellow grass. Elatrynn threw hat away and raised his sword. There was no time to attempt any magic. He sprang aside as the first beast attempted to trample him under its strange limbs. He blocked a falling blade, slashed at a stirrup, dived to the grass and rolled under the belly of another creature, stabbing wildly. As he sprang to his feet, he saw the Voidal standing motionless and uninvolved; somehow, none of the riders were coming close to him, leaving him out of the fight entirely.

"A hand here – if you're not too busy?" Elatrynn yelled. The Voidal gazed back, his expression quizzical. Another rider stabbed at Elatrynn and he grabbed the sword arm, yanking the rider from his saddle, kicking the bizarre helm as hard as he could. The mount's tusks slashed dismayingly close to Elatrynn's throat, beak snapping. He grabbed the reins and vaulted into the saddle, not pausing to wonder if he could master the beast.

Two more riders pressed him from left and right. Barely able to parry their combined attack, he let his mount do as it would. It reared in panic, almost throwing Elatrynn, and all but disembowelling the creature to its left. Free to concentrate on his right flank, Elatrynn smashed his sword hilt against the rider's helm, toppling him from the saddle. He grabbed at his new mount's reins and pulled back savagely. The beast instantly quieted, although it snarled a tooth-jarring whine, giving Elatrynn a moment to take stock. Three riders had lost their mounts, but each was already back on foot. That left two mounted, plus the one in blue and gold, whom Elatrynn assumed was their commander. Luck had been on his side up to now, he could no longer expect the riders to underestimate his sword and riding skills.

"Voidal! I really would appreciate a little help!"

"There is no need."

Elatrynn stared at the green-eyed man in disbelief. He was standing as motionless as before, but now his face bore a distracted, almost dreamy expression. "Meaning?"

The Voidal's expression cleared a little and he frowned, as though a train of thought had been broken. "There is no need," he repeated, although his voice no longer carried conviction.

"No need," Elatrynn murmured, his tone sour. But even as he spoke, his mind was racing through a catalogue of techniques and magical effects which, due to a certain lack of practice, he'd all but forgotten. "I was warned there'd be days like this."

One of the unseated riders was back in a saddle and had rejoined the three still mounted. All four charged. Elatrynn wheeled his mount and goaded it into a fast, loping run with the flat of his sword. Risking a glance over his shoulder he wondered if the gap between them was enough.

He rested the edge of his sabre against his mount's speckled neck. "Sorry about this," he breathed, and slashed the creature's throat.

The beast crashed to the yellow grass, front limbs collapsing like dry sticks. Elatrynn somersaulted awkwardly to the ground. He ran his tongue along the flat of his blade, gagging on the bitter taste of the creature's blood. He swallowed once, and croaked: "Now!"

The four riders were almost upon the twitching corpse. The hide convulsed; the dead thing lurched up onto its hind legs. Pale smoke dribbling from the wound in its neck, it lashed out with warped forelimbs. Talons the length of a man's arm dragged two riders from their mounts, shredding their armour. A mournful sound, like rending steel, came from the transforming creature's mouth. Ploughing furrows in the grass, it took a tentative step. It grew larger, more confident, with each new stride. Every bodily angle became exaggerated, teeth and claws grew impossibly long. It stalked the last two riders, blocking their retreat. Its original body was no more than tatters of hide hanging from gleaming black angles and razor-edged spikes. It cut riders and mounts apart with two negligent swipes of what had once been forelimbs. Sounding its despairing metallic shriek again, it made for the figures on foot.

Neither intended to suffer the fate of their comrades. They fled back over the hill whence Elatrynn had first spotted them. The thing pursued them to the brow, where it paused. It seemed uncertain, crooning to itself. After a moment it fell silent, its huge, angular form imploding.

Elatrynn came to his feet, leaning on his sword like an old man. The Voidal was approaching, holding Elatrynn's battered hat, expression betraying neither concern nor surprise.

"You were right – no need," wheezed Elatrynn. "I don't know what I could have been thinking..." He snatched his hat and jammed it on angrily.

The Voidal shook his head. "That was not my meaning. Help was near."

Elatrynn rubbed gingerly at the base of his spine. "Can't say I noticed."

"But you always were impatient, Marudwy."

Elatrynn wheeled at the sound of the new voice. A tall, painfully thin woman stood before him, leaning on a wooden staff even taller than she. Her clothing gave the impression of being patched together from a hundred ill-matching suits. A feathered cap, similarly motley, was perched over long greying hair which still held traces of its original red. Her eyes were a watery blue, caught in a net of laugh-lines. A huge, aquiline nose dominated her thin face.

For a moment Elatrynn refused to believe what he was seeing. Then he sheathed his sword, laughed and threw his arms around her bony shoulders. "Rhyma! I never thought I'd see you again! Not after the Veilworld…!" He stepped back, still holding her at arm's length. "You've not changed— Nothing—" His voice choked off.

Rhyma looked Elatrynn up and down. "That's more than I can say for you, Marudwy. Last time I saw you, you were half as tall and twice as insolent! By all the gods, it must be some time…!"

Elatrynn laughed again. "Ten thousand centuries and a hundred million worlds! At least, that's how it feels. And it's Elatrynn – for the moment, anyway. Marudwy was a naïve boy." He indicated his black-clothed companion. "And yonder cheerful fellow is the Voidal. He—"

"I am familiar with the Voidal." Rhyma stepped up to the Dark Man and stared at him frankly. "I had heard rumours that Fatecaster had escaped its quarantine. Naturally, I discounted them." After a moment she glanced back at Elatrynn, a thin smile on her lips. "And just as naturally, I find you in dubious company."

Elatrynn shrugged. "It's a long and boring story. You wouldn't care for it." His own smile fell away. "But what are you doing here? I thought nothing could drag you away from Erberow."

"And nothing can!" Rhyma was rueful. "Or so I'd thought. That was before I turned a corner in a favourite part of my garden, and found myself here!" She waved her long staff at the gentle landscape. "Where *is* here, by the way?"

"Ela'ancidor," said the Voidal, his voice distant.

"Where?" Elatrynn was unfamiliar with the name.

"We are no longer within your Infinite Tiers – not as such – nor some isolated realm such as my own Omniverse." The Voidal looked at them both directly, as though sure of something for the first time. He touched his skull with trembling fingers. "I feel it – I feel the difference. This is a place ... outside. And I know its name: Ela'ancidor."

Rhyma stamped her staff on the grass. "I knew I recognised that smell! Ela'ancidor! A damned Node World! Where Realities that are too dissimilar or antithetical even for the infinite variety of the Boundless may touch without mutual destruction."

Elatrynn frowned. "If that's true," he murmured, "then this could also be the home of one of the Nexus Jewels."

"Ah," sighed Rhyma. "Nexus Jewels." She rested her forehead on her tall staff. "I'm too old for this."

"The Jewel is in danger," the Voidal said. "Another has already been taken. Now the Jewel of Ela'ancidor is similarly threatened."

Elatrynn groaned. "So were our prettily-armoured friends trying to protect the Jewel? Or whoever wants to take it? They said something about the borders being sealed."

"At present, it lies in its chamber on an island which shares this world's name." The Voidal's right hand rose up and pointed, as if of its own volition. "That way," he added needlessly.

"You seem well versed in events." Rhyma's tone was light, but her meaning was clear.

"What would the Dark Gods want with a Nexus Jewel?" Elatrynn wondered aloud. "What would it gain them?"

"Who can divine the Dark Gods' motives?" murmured the Voidal. "Everything is a game to them. Action and reason frequently appear to contradict, or simply be nonsensical."

Rhyma dug her staff into the strange turf. "That's gods for you. I suspect they're all mad. But I suppose it's incumbent upon us to make for this island."

Elatrynn shrugged. "I had nothing else planned."

"I am most definitely too old for this." Rhyma began to stride easily across the undulating landscape.

❦❦❦

DESPITE HER OUTWARD manner, Rhyma was deeply concerned by the nature of this ill-judged quest. She knew Elatrynn – it was so hard not to think of him as Marudwy – would be relishing the danger, the uncertainty, the whole unpredictable novelty. It was that very recklessness which had led to his eventual self-imposed exile in the mortal worlds. Rhyma had no love for the aloof immortals who populated the Astral Tiers, but she much preferred to hide in her pastoral delights of Erberow. The affairs of humanity, who were born, grew old and died faster than the most transitory blooms in her gardens, interested her not at all. She had never understood the boy's attraction.

She smiled crookedly, thinking of all the rescued souls who lived in Erberow's tranquil freedom. No – that was entirely different!

And this Voidal, sometimes called Fatecaster after the sword he carried but never used. Rhyma recognised him from legend. Even in remote Erberow she'd caught rumours that somewhere a barrier within the more murky quarters of the Boundless was broached, allowing the Dark Man through. To be truthful, she was surprised some Celestials hadn't already intervened and ejected him like the poisonous infection he was. Perhaps they were too preoccupied with this threat to the Nexus Jewels.

Or perhaps they – Elatrynn and herself – were the Source's manner of dealing with the threat.

Rhyma shivered, though she wasn't cold. That was not a pretty thought.

She stepped over shreds of hide draping a scatter of crushed bones, all that remained of the mount Elatrynn had transformed. She was impressed: a phoenix conjuration. The boy she remembered could do little more than raise maggots from rotting flesh. He'd learnt some impressive tricks since then.

Rhyma toed the remains. They now looked nothing more than the desiccated remains of the dead mount, but she'd seen the transformed beast. A thing of sharp, metallic edges; almost feline. A gleaming lion of honed brass and iron. Why? Why hadn't Elatrynn simply taken the original form and made it bigger, deadlier?

She shook her head, told himself she was being a foolish old woman. She'd endured many a strange dream in her long existence. The recurrent dream which had lately plagued her – of a huge cat-like creature stalking through the Boundless, along warped corridors – was just a coincidence.

Elatrynn had halted, arm raised in warning. Ahead, something that might have been the result of a union between a scorpion and a particularly ugly fish was poised on a grassy rise. Its multi-limbed body was translucent; the brazen sun of Ela'ancidor refracted through it, striking a fiery glow. It raised two of its chitinous legs and felt the air. Rhyma readied her staff, noting that Elatrynn had already drawn his black rapier. The thing was hesitant, perhaps more afraid of them than they were of it. It lowered its limbs, drumming uncertainly on the ground before backing away. It raised a tall, webbed stinger as it retreated: an obvious warning. Rhyma was quite happy to treat it with all of the respect it demanded.

They waited for it to crawl out of sight before continuing. Cresting a hill Rhyma blinked, convinced her eyes were mistaken. The landscape – yellow hills, valleys, even the few clouds – seemed to be converging at a point on the horizon. She didn't think it was simply an illusion, for just visible at that vanishing point was a purple blotch. A building of some kind? A city? Or was it a shoreline, and the smudge an island?

And at the foot of the hill was a lone figure.

Elatrynn had clearly spotted the figure. "Company."

"One of those riders?" Rhyma mused, thinking it unlikely even as she spoke.

"No." The Voidal was unnervingly certain. "Another traveller. He

... she—" His voice tailed off. "No – it fades..."

"I wish your damned memory would be consistent," grumbled Elatrynn. "It's unnerving."

"There's something not so pleasingly familiar about that traveller," Rhyma commented. The dark silhouette, the arrogant stance, the aura of undying patience. She did not welcome the sudden recognition. "It's an Inquisitor."

Elatrynn looked at her, eyes troubled. "Any idea which one?"

"Does it matter? They're all bad omens." For some reason, she was reminded of her recurrent dream.

"Some more than others." Elatrynn nodded towards the Voidal, who was continuing down the hillside, unconcerned. "Think they've come for our friend there?"

"More likely it's here for exactly the same reason as ourselves." Rhyma sighed, suddenly feeling tired. "Whatever *that* is."

"Then maybe they'll be good enough to tell us." Elatrynn strode down in the Voidal's wake, towards the patient figure.

"Not sure I want to know," muttered Rhyma softly. Against her better judgement, she hurried after them both.

By the time Rhyma had caught them up she was within clear sight of the Inquisitor. She felt a faint sense of relief as she recognised them. Not the worst, then.

Typically, the Inquisitor's body was covered in dark material that seemed to emit a black radiance. A single, narrow-bladed sword hung across their slender back, a black staff not unlike Rhyma's own clutched in bony hands. Long hair of a delicate shade of blue crowned a narrow, angular face, with cold, slanting blue eyes above high sharp cheekbones. A smile that held no humour or welcome tugged at full, bloodless lips.

"Inquisitor Arqyell." Rhyma saluted the Inquisitor with full ceremony, bowing with a deference which owed more to wariness than respect. "Greetings."

"Duchess Ellyn of Erberow." The Inquisitor barely nodded their head in acknowledgement. The cold eyes flickered over the two men, turning into black, self-righteous anger as they fell upon the Voidal. "Marudwy – our paths cross again. And this would be the creature known as Fatecaster?"

"You know I prefer Rhyma to all that Duchess nonsense," Rhyma said in mild reproof.

"And most recently I've taken to Elatrynn." He folded his arms. "Now, perhaps you'd be good enough to explain our presence. We've had taunting hints, courtesy of the Voidal's failing memory, and a few threats. Added to which, none of us are here voluntarily."

Arqyell frowned. "Drawn here against your wills? Someone is playing at puppet master, it seems."

Elatrynn pulled a face. "In that we are agreed. But it's no explanation."

"We will walk as I explain." Arqyell set off towards the purple blot on the horizon before anyone could answer, black staff stabbing feverishly at the ground. "The Nexus Jewel of Ela'ancidor is under threat. From whence comes that danger is uncertain, but there has been a concurrent loss of another Jewel, elsewhere in the Internection. It cannot be coincidental."

"And that is why you are here?" Elatrynn's tone was disingenuous.

"In part. I am also seeking—" Arqyell paused, as though reluctant to continue. "A colleague," they concluded eventually.

"Another Inquisitor?" Rhyma's disquiet returned: that tall black staff was too familiar. It was not, she thought, Arqyell's. "Might I enquire which one?"

"You may enquire, certainly."

The Inquisitor added nothing more. Rhyma knew she'd had all the answers she was likely to receive. "Has it occurred to anyone that – much as I loathe the term – we are all Eternals?" she asked, changing tack. She was growing breathless, even her long legs were struggling to keep up with Arqyell's stride. "With the exception of Fatecaster, here. And even he can no longer claim to be truly mortal."

"Your point, your grace?" asked Arqyell.

"Rhyma—!"

"It's obvious," Elatrynn said. He looked troubled. "Whenever two dwellers from the Astral Tiers combine their potential, the results are greater than the individual parts. And for each additional Eternal, the increase in potential is exponential. Even without the Voidal, you know what we three alone could accomplish."

Arqyell's voice trailed back. "Someone else has also considered this."

Rhyma had stopped listening. She was relieved Elatrynn had spotted the possibilities, not at all surprised that Arqyell had also. Her attention was fixed upon the distant smudge towards which they were heading. They seemed to be nearing it considerably faster than made sense. Almost as if it too was moving – and in their direction. It was taking on a shape: resolving from a misty, amorphous blot into a huge, slate-coloured oval. Wedged between the hills, it blocked their way. A towering stone head, the eyes fashioned to stare intimidatingly down at anyone approaching.

For a moment, Rhyma imagined it was the head of a titanic cat, a heartbeat later, it was in the shape of a man's face. An oddly familiar face. A few more steps, during which time it seemed to rush towards them ever faster, and Rhyma knew why.

She turned to Elatrynn. By his expression she knew that he had also recognised it. "It's you."

"No," said Elatrynn coldly. "That's my father's face."

Rhyma reassessed the massive features. The face had no beard, true, but that aside, it was still Elatrynn's face. She forced her memory back, to before Marudwy's birth. When she had been partly responsible for the resurrection of a dead human sorcerer into something godlike. Elatrynn's father, who as a mortal had gone by the name Daryed.

"Of course." She was overawed, apprehensive of what the sculpture meant. "How did you know?"

Elatrynn spoke quietly. "For a while, on that world which my father had created and shielded from the Internection, I was filled with his soul. Daryed and Marudwy were briefly the same creature." He took a step forward. "And it is also the face of the one who, for his own ends, helped resurrect my father after he died."

The titanic sculpture leapt into clearer focus. Rhyma finally saw what Elatrynn had already made out: it was clearly not just one face. Its features were composed of smaller faces, and they of ones smaller yet.

"Shilnoth," she said. The second player in that ancient drama, whose tainted gift had been Daryed's immortality. "Someone has a bizarre sense of humour."

Arqyell shrugged. "This is Ela'ancidor: a Node World beyond causality. Each realm containing a Nexus Jewel resonates with events from other realities."

The Voidal spoke. "And may provide a gateway to those realities."

Rhyma had almost forgotten the Dark Man's presence. She tried to penetrate those green eyes, guess what thoughts must be passing through the gaunt skull. "Such as a way back to your – how is it called? Omniverse?"

The Voidal barely nodded. "I should not be in this reality," he said quietly. "Even here, effectively in a neutral zone, I can feel what you refer to as the Boundless trying to reject me. To thrust me back to my own corner of damnation" He looked at them all, in turn, his expression frank, almost pleading. "Perhaps that is why I was drawn here. To return."

"Unless your masters have designs on the Jewel," Elatrynn suggested. "You admit you have no idea of their motives."

The Voidal lowered his head. "No," he agreed, voice barely audible.

Elatrynn threw up his hands and grinned. "Well, who wants to live forever!" He turned back towards the huge face-wall, and his face paled. "Gods and hellfire!" he whispered.

Rhyma couldn't understand why no one had seen it happen. As they'd been speaking, the slate-grey edifice had shifted to within an arm's length of where they stood. Now, looking up, she could no longer make out the features, it was just a towering wall covered in a mosaic of gargoyle faces, themselves a swirl of yet smaller faces. Rhyma had no doubt that the pattern repeated endlessly until everything was too small to be visible.

Arqyell cried a warning: "It's opening up!"

Agonising light speared Rhyma's eyes, lancing her brain. Unable to see or cry out, her consciousness was rent apart and drowned.

⁂

THE VOIDAL STOOD blind and immobile as fury erupted around him. White-hot brilliance filled his mind, his eyes. It was, he imagined, like standing at the heart of a new-born star. But for all the world about him churned, he was largely untouched. He was little more than a spectator, allowed to witness great events, never to be part of them. Was this, he wondered, because he was from outside this continuum, immune to its ravages. Or was it the hand of the Dark Gods, shielding him; leaving him free to proceed with whatever plan they had in mind.

He pressed gauntleted palms against his eyes, wishing futilely for some fragment of his true memory, and the freedom of choice it might allow him.

As though it had been waiting for that one thought, the storm changed. No longer screaming harmlessly around him, it tore into his body, splitting flesh that was no longer a barrier. A soul-freezing hurricane swirled deep into his fibre, filling the hollowness that was the Voidal.

His head was crowded with images, memories: deeds past, deeds present, deeds future. Acts which should never have been committed, actions that should never have followed. A million lifetimes' memories; all true, all fiction, all his. They tore him in a way the external chaos could not. The howling went on and on, but the storm had dissipated, swallowed by the nothingness where once had been his soul. The only sounds were the Voidal's screams of denial.

Flinging gaunt arms around his shoulders, the Dark Man sank to his knees. Although his eyes were open, he could not see past the endless visions and false memories which seethed behind them.

"Was that meant to be a deterrent," came a voice to his left, "or a way in?"

The voice was familiar, it reminded him of … of—? So many names and faces crowded his thoughts that the Voidal couldn't concentrate. To have so much information was no better than none at all.

"It was to ensure our arrival." The Voidal felt the words moving his lips, impatient to be released. He had no control over them. "This is where we should be."

"I knew it!" came a second voice. It too released a plague of images the Voidal couldn't assimilate. "We're just puppets!"

"What's the matter, Rhyma?" came the first voice again: warm, ironic. It provoked an unfamiliar response in the Voidal. "Don't you like being on the receiving end for once?"

"Very funny," said the voice of the one called Rhyma. "I was on the receiving end of your tricks often enough. It palls after a while, I assure you."

"Something appears to be wrong with that creature," came a third voice: cold, assertive. The thoughts and faces awakened by those words dragged an involuntary shudder from the Voidal.

There were more words; none of them mattered. He was slipping deeper into the pandemonium of other lives, other dreams. He would drown soon, he knew, become nothing more than a vessel filled with others' pasts. The thought held a grain of comfort. If the Voidal could no longer have his own memories, he would be content with proxies.

"Get him onto his feet at least." Those words cut through all the vying thoughts. A moment later, he was gripped under the arms and pulled upright. He assumed there was some form of ground under his feet – for he seemed to be standing, after a fashion – but he couldn't feel it.

More words formed out of the maelstrom in his brain: "What's the matter with him?" Who was saying that? And when?

"Elfloq?" The word meant nothing. Perhaps it made sense to one of his voices.

"If he was still human, I'd say he was delirious."

"Place his hands on this—"

The Voidal might have screamed his throat raw at the sudden, all-consuming torment. He could not be sure. Liquid pain drenched his arms. Every nerve ending burned and died in exquisite agony. And with each small death, a lost, hopeless life flared and was gone.

His tear-filled eyes could see again. Anaesthetic void numbed the pain, the loss, once more. A hollow man straightened his still trembling body and nodded. "Yes," he said, his voice so distant. Already he was forgetting the agony of memory, and the agony of loss. The Voidal looked at the three faces staring intently at his own. All showed a form of compassion, each after their own fashion. He was so empty, even that was seized upon gratefully.

He glanced down at his hands – so ordinary, grasping a black staff. He frowned: surely that was wrong. Did he not have—? The mayfly thought evaded him, a moment later, he had forgotten even that.

The Inquisitor – Arqyell – took the staff away. It disturbed the Voidal, evoking strange images of its own. His left hand was seized with a brief palsy, it didn't want to release the staff.

"I am grateful," he said, dropping empty hands to his side. And then he felt them again: phantom whispers at the back of his mind, tiny pieces of causality, tenuous shadows of the future. So, he wasn't to be entirely alone.

"May we proceed, then?" That was Rhyma, her long face pulled thinner by obvious distaste. The Dark Man was unmoved. Had he memory or feelings left, he would still have been used to such a reaction.

"I'll follow your beaming smile, sour bones." This was Elatrynn, who sparked a curious sensation in the Voidal's mind. Was it warmth? Friendship? He knew the terms, but had little understanding of their meaning.

Arqyell said nothing. The swirling ideas in the Voidal's head shrank away from the Inquisitor. He didn't need their prompting to fear them, but he yearned to know why.

Finally, the Voidal took in their surroundings. They were beyond the bizarre wall, or inside it. Although he saw no obvious roof or ceiling, still there was the sense of being enclosed. Buildings clustered around them, of every architectural style and fancy, many unfinished. Grandiose palaces of reeds or paper perched atop delicate spun-glass towers, rustic cottages of some granular material that was in constant motion festered in gassy bogs, gothic castles sprawled around black hills or still lakes, empty tower blocks of gold and diamonds crumbled amidst scorched wastelands. Everywhere was draped with clots of something that looked as dense as moss, but had no more substance than gossamer. A sourceless, pallid light filled every corner, making the townscape flat and unreal. Nowhere, beyond the four of them, was there a sign of life.

"Cheerful little town," remarked Rhyma, kicking at the base of a castle's tower. It crumbled, having no more cohesion than dry, grey sand.

"There is very little of the real or objective in a Node World," said Arqyell. "The worlds beyond overlap. Even our own hopes and aspirations can affect what we see here."

"There's precious little hope evident in this sorry crop of buildings," commented Elatrynn. He ran a finger across a paper wall; it collapsed into sour dust.

The Inquisitor was thoughtful. "Almost as though there is a negative pressure: Ela'ancidor sucking in the despair and shattered dreams of the Boundless."

The Voidal was silent, remembering the desperation and betrayal that had filled him.

"If that's true," Elatrynn was saying, "then it's a deliberate act. Even allowing for leakage, no interface pattern should be like this."

"Agreed." Arqyell pointed their staff down a bleak street. "Somewhere there will be life. And our answer."

The Voidal hesitated as Rhyma and Elatrynn fell in behind the Inquisitor. In the end he had no choice but to follow: that way lay his only chance of returning home. But his feelings, the conflicting thoughts swimming in his brain, urged him to flee. To be away as far and as fast as he could. Silently protesting every step, he followed them anyway.

Their footsteps should have echoed. The ghastly silence all around absorbed what little sound they made, leaving them as dark ghosts moving through a bleached landscape. It added a further dab of unreality to a scene from which the Voidal felt hopelessly divorced. Spurious images would flicker at odd moments, superimposing themselves over what he saw. As though he were witnessing a whole universe of consequences from each tiny act of choice.

Elatrynn sniffed at the air. "Can you smell the sea?"

After a moment Arqyell nodded in agreement. "Quite near."

Rhyma snorted. "You've both gone daft. I can't smell a thing."

"The Sea of Bynedd." Certain knowledge filled the Voidal an instant before he spoke. "It laps the shores of Ela'ancidor and stretches out to—" For a moment, he thought the fragile memory would fade.

"Paradise, perhaps?" Rhyma sneered.

"No – Infinity." The Voidal sighed, wondering how he could convey what he knew in something so crude as words. "Bynedd is ceaseless. It goes—" he shrugged, knowing the words sounded too simple; too trite "—everywhere."

"And you think we're going to pop you on a boat and let you sail back to your Omniverse?" Rhyma continued. "Is that why we're here, eh? To escort you back to your masters?"

"Gently," murmured Elatrynn. "You know that isn't that case."

"Well...!" Rhyma threw up her hands in disgust and stalked off, maliciously cracking her long staff against fragile walls.

"Elatrynn!" Arqyell's tone was so urgent that the Voidal was also compelled to turn. The Inquisitor was pointing with their own staff down a narrow, precarious street. "Something!"

For a moment, the Voidal saw nothing but curiously monochrome buildings, then a shape flickered against a wall. Dark and feline, the shadow cast by something unseen slunk across the pale street, and vanished. The image of a face – pale, green-eyed, implacable – filled the Voidal's head. It was a face he found himself dreading even more than Arqyell's.

"No," he mumbled. "I will not do it! I cannot—!"

"WELCOME ALL! HOW GLAD WE ARE TO SEE YOU AGAIN!"

The thundering voice belled around the motley collection of buildings, filling the spaces between them. A few shuddered at the volume, shedding fragments of rotting shell. Chunks of the gossamer moss blew away as though in a hurricane.

Elatrynn was looking about, his face tense. "Again? I think you have the advantage of us, sir—"

"NONSENSE, MARUDWY – YOU'RE JUST BEING MODEST. SURELY YOU MUST RECOGNISE US. AFTER ALL, WE'VE BARELY JUST PARTED. AND INQUISITOR ARQYELL TOO."

A delicate glass column shattered, the rambling cottage it supported fell into dust. Blue-grey walls spun into the air and flew away: millions of jewelled flies.

The Voidal listened intently to his internal voices; strangely they gave no clue to the newcomer.

Rhyma rejoined them, her face flushed. "Did you hear that?"

"Hard not to," remarked Elatrynn. "Do you recognise the voice?"

"One of the gods?" she wondered. "It's loud and self-important enough. Yet there is something familiar about it."

"That's no god—"

"*YOU THINK NOT, MARUDWY?*" the voice interrupted. "*WE BELIEVE IT'S ALL A MATTER OF PERSPECTIVE...*"

Elatrynn raised his head, black eyes distant. "You lost your perspective back on the Veilworld, Shilnoth," he said quietly. "What a pity it wasn't your life..."

The voice erupted into a spiteful howl. The Voidal tried in vain to block his ears. The three with him did the same, as all about them the facsimile township flew apart into dust and rags. When the debris had cleared a throne stood in the centre of the scoured wasteland. Something sat on the throne: something that changed its shape and colour with every heartbeat. The Voidal's eyes ached if he looked at it for too long.

"Very well, we welcome you all again," said Shilnoth, his voice low and seductive. "A pity you had to spoil the game so soon, Marudwy. We had hoped to enjoy your confusion a while longer. Ah, well." He waved a tendril that became a shelled limb. "However, we do not recall meeting this before." Shilnoth glared at the Voidal with eyes that shifted size and shape and hue faster and faster. "What is *it* doing here?"

"More to the point, Shilnoth—" said Arqyell, black staff waving generally in the shapeless being's direction, "—what are you doing here?"

"A small matter of a Nexus Jewel, if I know him," commented Rhyma.

"Ambition always was a peculiar characteristic with you," remarked Elatrynn. "Almost human, in fact."

Shilnoth began to laugh, the sound turning to a phlegmy hiss as his mouth atrophied. Just as swiftly, it became a pouting bud of orange petals. "We prefer to see it as more … godlike."

Rhyma rubbed her large nose. "How strange. Most gods would prefer never to see you again."

"Enjoy your joke, hag." Shilnoth's ever-changing body grew translucent, and then transparent. "It may bring you comfort in the unchanging eternity which awaits you here—" The throne was empty; after a moment it, too, crumpled.

"I think we can assume it wasn't him brought us hither." Rhyma hawked and spat into the thin dust that covered the ground.

"True enough." Elatrynn scratched his beard and looked at the Voidal. The Dark Man didn't know what was expected of him, and kept his silence. "Why expend all that energy dragging us here just to put on a loud voice yet do nothing?" He shifted his gaze to Arqyell. "Shilnoth may not be rational, but I don't think he's so foolish."

"Unless he's already tapped the Nexus Jewel," said Rhyma. "He could afford any number of pointless gestures then."

"No," said the Voidal with unfamiliar certainty. "The Shapeless One has so far failed to access the Jewel, and our sudden appearance has alarmed him."

"Could have fooled me," muttered Rhyma.

"If Shilnoth had that power, he would undoubtedly use it," said

Arqyell. "It was to seize Daryed's soul-force that led him to trick Rhyma and the young Marudwy into uncovering the Veilworld." The Inquisitor sighed. "First an all-powerful ring, now a Nexus Jewel. His methods become more ambitious, even as the ambition remains the same."

As though Arqyell's words brought sudden order to the Voidal's chaotic mind, he saw it. A play acted out by stuttering marionettes, time disjointed and uneven.

—A human sorcerer, Daryed: standing dwarfed and lost in a court that flickers and warps as fast as its shapeless liege. Shilnoth gifting him a crimson Soul Ring of unbelievable power.

—Daryed: dying, betrayed. Lost despite the Soul Ring's power.

—Death driven back: the ring flows into Daryed, possessing him. A tall, skeletal woman dressed all in motley plays an unusually long flute as the rite consummates. The sorcerer becomes the ring incarnate.

—Daryed: a demi-god, driven by vengeance. Destroying his enemies, levelling his world in unquenchable anger. Consumed by guilt, loathing what he has become, wrenching what little of his world survives free of the Boundless. Guarding it from even the gods' interference by the power of his metempsychotic soul. The Veilworld.

—The final battle: Shilnoth attempting to sublimate that power into himself, opposed by the boy Marudwy, and Rhyma. The moment when Marudwy briefly absorbs his lost father's soul-force, exorcising Shilnoth in one incandescent gesture. The Veilworld dropping beyond the Boundless one last time; safe from both Shilnoth and the gods' meddling, screened by what had once been Daryed—

The images faded. The Voidal sighed. "Shilnoth will possess the

Veilworld. The Sea of Bynedd can be made to flow there too. Once he has secured the Jewel, he will efface the Veilworld and torment the immortal spark of Daryed forever. Simple revenge." His shoulders slumped. "The Shapeless One is, after all, a shallow creature."

"And also unpredictable." Elatrynn was gazing around the razed collection of buildings. "You can see the effect of an unbalanced mind."

"Something yonder seems to have escaped." Rhyma gestured with her staff. A mirage of razor edged towers, floating balconies and domes shimmered like heat haze. Beyond it, something broad and flat glittered.

"That must be the city," said Arqyell. "The closest Ela'ancidor can come to independent creation."

Elatrynn nodded. "Explaining why it escaped Shilnoth's little tantrum."

"And beyond it the Sea of Bynedd." The Voidal could feel it drawing him relentlessly, the city before it a focus of both his need and intangible dread. "Our journey is almost at an end."

"All roads lead to Bynedd, eh?" Elatrynn's mood was jaunty once more. "And at the end of our quest, a Jewel to beat all jewels."

"And some answers," grumbled Rhyma. "I'm getting too old for all this intrigue."

"So you keep saying." Elatrynn favoured them all with his widest grin. "Shall I lead?"

"To where?" asked Arqyell. "The city has come to us."

Even though he was confident he had never taken his eyes from it, the Voidal never saw the city move. One moment it had been far away, the next they were a few steps from its closest towers, Bynedd along with it. Perhaps it was they who had moved, or been drawn closer. The Voidal shook his head: such concepts didn't apply in Ela'ancidor. Things were as they were.

The armoured figures appeared before them in much the same way as the city. Like those the Voidal and Elatrynn had encountered on first arriving, their armour was bizarrely-fashioned and gaudy. And as before, they moved and acted like automatons.

"Return whence you came," said the closest in a colourless voice.

Elatrynn drew his sword. "Haven't we gone through all this before?"

"Are they fully corporeal?" Arqyell lowered their black staff to the ground. "There is something about them. Something missing." The Inquisitor drew their sword.

"They are soulless." The Voidal recognised the familiarity. "The Shapeless One has sucked them dry, used their spirit as nourishment I—" his fists clenched with a passion alien to him "—feel for them."

"This is not exactly the time for altruism," remarked Elatrynn.

"Return whence you have come," insisted the armoured figure, flat voice barely raised above a monotone.

"Oh hellfire and gods' blessings!" swore Rhyma. "I've had enough of this!" She strode forward, swinging her staff. One blow against the gaudy helm crushed it almost flat. The figure collapsed like a stringless marionette.

The remaining figures drew their unfamiliar weapons, moving forward in unison. It was barely a charge. The Voidal noted that, once again, the armoured figures treated him as though he were invisible.

To his left, Arqyell hacked a figure down, leapt elegantly over the falling corpse and ran a second through. On his right, Elatrynn – hatless again – fenced enthusiastically with three bemused guards. Before him, an enraged Rhyma bludgeoned her way. The Voidal followed in their wake.

Within moments all four were inside the city. The distant urging in the Voidal's mind became a frantic scream. His skull throbbed with its urgency. He could not mistake the direction: it was clearer than any beacon.

"This way. The Nexus Chamber." Not waiting to see if his three companions followed, he made unsteadily towards the summons.

The city passed him like a dream. He saw nothing of the buildings he must have walked by, the passageways. Only the call was real. Of all the possible futures that danced behind his eyes, only one contained that voice: painfully clear, sharper than any blade. He was only remotely aware of Elatrynn, Rhyma and Arqyell behind him, struggling to match his desperate pace.

The call was his only reality.

He almost ran into the wall in his blindness. He stood helpless before it, palms running over its smooth, gently curved surface. The desperate cry was coming from inside! He must get in! He was needed. So needed!

"What's through there?"

Elatrynn's voice came from behind him. The Voidal pounded on the wall with a gloved hand. It chimed faintly. "The Nexus Chamber. I must get in!"

"Why would Shilnoth build a solid wall around the very thing he covets?" Rhyma's tone was frankly sceptical.

"Because it also contains something the Shapeless One wishes to imprison." Arqyell held up the black staff. The Voidal heard its keening: an almost animal intensity.

The Inquisitor pressed an ear against the shaft. "They are here!"

"Who is here?" demanded Rhyma. The Voidal shared the thin woman's obvious concern.

Arqyell struck the wall with the staff's brazen tip. The smooth surface fragmented into a spider web of cracks, disintegrating a moment later. Not a mote of dust remained.

"Inquisitor Uryell!" Arqyell stepped through into a wide compartment. Before them, a bright, flickering light outlined a further doorway. "Uryell!"

"I should have guessed!" hissed Rhyma. "Uryell of the Gra'al." She struck the floor with her own staff. "I hate cats!"

The Voidal barely understood. "You are old friends?"

"Hardly! Our paths have seldom crossed. That Inquisitor isn't known for their forgiving nature. A stern guardian of orthodoxy – or what they perceive as the orthodox – adept at rooting out heresies wherever they choose to find them. Hiding myself away in Erberow, letting the Boundless go to hell, might be viewed as more than dangerously eccentric." Rhyma clutched her staff tight in whitening hands.

The Voidal understood. After all, was he not the most unorthodox creature present?

A figure that might have been Arqyell's twin stood against the doorway's flickering outline, though it looked tired and drained.

Although alike in clothing, the steely blue of Arqyell's eyes and hair was replaced in the newcomer by slit-pupiled, feline eyes of dull green, and long hair of a striking red.

Arqyell dropped to one knee, the black staff held out reverentially. "Lord Uryell, I return your *mandra'al* staff. It was found alone in a lifeless, non-contiguous Tier *abjacent* to the Wild Precincts."

Uryell raised a rune-covered metal arm. Retractable pincers closed around the staff's shaft. A spark of renewed vitality flickered in the green eyes. The Inquisitor straightened. They examined the staff curiously, especially the silver-gold tips. "Was it damaged in any way?"

"The *mandra'al* was unhurt, Lord Uryell, thank the Source."

Uryell grunted and spun the black staff. They seemed satisfied.

Arqyell stood. "Has Shilnoth treated you well?"

Uryell's gaze flickered across the rescuers, resting briefly on the Voidal. The Dark Man tensed as their eyes widened in brief recognition. He didn't believe this creature's close attentions were in his best interest.

"No less than he dared. In truth I do not believe my presence factored in his plans: it was the *mandra'al* he coveted."

Arqyell frowned. "Then we have brought him exactly what he wished for."

With a twist of their pincers, Uryell spun the black staff. "Perhaps. On Barofonn he had a Nexus Jewel, yet I defeated him – though it cost us both dearly. Here in this Nexus Chamber I am powerless, yet together I think we have the weapons to defeat him."

The Nexus Chamber! The Voidal felt the mental pull double in strength. Through the light-filled doorway! He must go!

A black staff snapped out, blocking his way. A fraction closer and it would have shattered his neck. "I think not," said Uryell softly.

"I must!" pleaded the Voidal. He was almost sobbing: torn between the awful desperation of the call in his head and his fear of this implacable, green-eyed creature. "Otherwise the Islands ... when they rise... We must...!"

"Lord Inquisitor!" came Elatrynn's voice. "We must trust him."

"And what do you know of when the Islands rise?" Uryell demanded.

The Voidal couldn't look away from those hard green eyes. He shook his head. "Nothing—" He rubbed at his temple. "The thoughts come and go..."

Uryell stared a moment longer at the Voidal, then looked towards Elatrynn. "Very well. But it's our lives if you are wrong – and you will precede us all, Marudwy." The sensuous mouth twitched with a smile that owed nothing to humour.

"Elatrynn," he insisted.

Uryell shrugged and lowered their staff. "As you wish. Rhyma, Elatrynn: you will enter the chamber first; Fatecaster shall follow. Arqyell and I will be last. Whatever either of us demands, you will all obey, instantly!"

"I liked you better when you were weakened," mumbled Rhyma.

In order, all five stepped towards the door. It slid open readily, as though awaiting them. A huge sapphire pulsed in the centre of the chamber, surrounded on three sides by tall windows overlooking the Bynedd Sea. Five rocky outcrops, jutting from the calm ocean, formed a rough semi-circle just beyond the shore. Uryell stepped up to the Nexus Jewel, running a hand over its bright surface.

"I suggest you hurry," called Elatrynn. He was standing at the open doorway, rapier ready. His entire body looked drawn tight enough to snap.

The Voidal moved to one of the windows, peering out at the ragged peaks jutting from the water. His mind whirled: images of the past, present, and many possible futures once again battled for dominance. He leaned heavily against the clear crystal with his left hand, not daring to take his right arm from under his cloak.

There was a clash of arms. Two grotesquely-armoured men stepped through the doorway. Elatrynn sprang at one, his sword flicking between helm and gorget. The guard went down soundlessly, gaudy armour spraying purple blood.

Rhyma whirled her long staff and smashed the end against the second guard's helm. The metal buckled like paper; underneath something snapped, audible even above the Jewel's electric hum. The guard's body folded.

"Uryell!" urged Elatrynn.

The Inquisitor glared at him before returning to a slow, careful scrutiny of the Jewel. "Elatrynn! Your sword!" Uryell held out a hand.

The other looked sadly at his rapier. "Must I?"

"Do it!" Uryell's relentless eyes hardened further. Elatrynn shrugged in resignation, and tossed his sword across.

"Voidal!" the Inquisitor ordered. At the sound of his name he focused his eyes on the pulsing Jewel, seeing a hundred overlaid Uryells in the facets.

"Stand on my right!" one of the shades commanded. Other lips mouthed different words: mute puppets from other dramas. "Take the sword!"

Like one caught in an inescapable nightmare, the Voidal reached out his left hand. It closed around the rapier's basket hilt. Uryell laid their right hand over the top – the Voidal would never be able to release his grip. Together they guided the sword point towards the centre of the Jewel.

"Touch the Nexus with your right hand," ordered the Inquisitor.

The Voidal tried to recoil, but Uryell's grip held him tight. "No!" Terror consumed him. "Do you know what you are asking?"

"Do it! Or surely we shall all perish!"

"We may all perish anyway—!" His voice choked off as he felt his right hand twitch. Powerless, he watched it rise from under his cloak, edging towards the Jewel.

A dazzling radiance filled the chamber. An unbearable brilliance. The Voidal stared at the incandescent thing which grew from his wrist. This was not what he had expected; what he'd feared. No easier to look upon than the core of a star, there was no hand. Indeed, there seemed to be nothing solid beyond the aching light.

It thrust itself at the Nexus Jewel. Invisible fingers pressed into the gem. Waves of spectral light infected the sapphire depths. The Voidal stared as Uryell raised the *mandra'al* staff, touching it against the Jewel's surface. It entered as though encountering nothing harder than molasses.

A deep throb resonated from within the huge gem. Waves of colour rose from its core, breaking against the facets. Chanting words that made no sense to the Voidal, Uryell forced Elatrynn's rapier into the stone's heart. Silence, cold as the depths of space, enveloped the chamber. Only Elatrynn's voice, an infinity away, could be heard:

"The Islands are rising!"

❦❦❦

RHYMA HURRIED TO Elatrynn's side at the windows. "Hellfire!" she muttered. Her voice was tinny, distant. "That's a sight! What d'you think started that?"

Elatrynn watched the five rocky peaks as they grew out of an increasingly restless Sea of Bynedd. "Uryell! Voidal! Whatever you need to do, might I suggest you do it quickly!"

He glanced back towards the Jewel, shocked by what he saw. Both the Inquisitor and Dark Man were engulfed in crystalline flames. They were nothing more than outcrops of the silently burning Nexus Jewel.

For the first time, Elatrynn entertained the idea that he was going to fail. He was going to die: to cease utterly. In that instant, he understood why his fellow Eternals so despised mortals and their immortal souls. To exist beyond death – somehow. Who wouldn't desire that—?

"Marudwy!"

He looked towards the doorway and that detested voice. Shilnoth, his restless shape made more nightmarish by the flickering Jewel-light, limped towards him. Elatrynn burned in pure hatred. His sword was gone, even his innate magic was nothing against Shilnoth. During their last encounter the young Marudwy had been filled with the power of the Soul Ring, and he'd been able to do nothing more than exorcize the Shapeless One from the Veilworld.

"Come to gloat, worm-flesh?" His voice, even in the chamber's unnatural quiet, was muffled.

"Gloat!" Shilnoth hobbled closer. Elatrynn realised part of his body was paralyzed, no longer ceaselessly morphing. "You invade this chamber and corrupt the Jewel!" He waved upper limbs in a grotesque pantomime. "Do you know why we have been so cautious? What happens when that Jewel is attacked? The Islands rise!"

"What of it?" Elatrynn's fingers were itching to rip Shilnoth apart. If only he would come within reach—

"We do not know!" Shilnoth was almost plaintive. "But they will destroy the city, and us with it. Only the Jewel can survive!"

"Seems fair to me."

"No!" Rhyma sprang away from the window, her staff raised. She smashed it into Shilnoth's head before he could react. With a scream, Shilnoth fell prone upon the floor, limbs cradling a wound that, uncharacteristically, did not heal. Rhyma straddled the fallen creature, staff raised again. "If only I'd destroyed you on the Veilworld."

Shilnoth's head turned slightly. "All roads lead to Ela'ancidor." His voice was mocking.

"Rhyma!" Elatrynn felt as though his loudest scream could never penetrate the crushing silence. *"Rhyma!"*

Shilnoth's head turned a little more, and more still. Owl-like, it rotated one hundred and eighty degrees. Before Rhyma could strike, the Shapeless One's twisted features leered an ever-changing grin. "From the Veilworld to a Node World. A completed circle; a single road. Goodbye, Ellyn of Erberow."

Shilnoth's body erupted straight up in a column of flesh. He enfolded Rhyma, crushing her. From somewhere deep within that churning bag there was a final, enraged cry. Then Shilnoth recoiled, his plastic form snapping back to the floor. Rhyma's mangled frame stood for a moment, before sinking to the ground: a boneless ruin.

At first, Elatrynn could not absorb what he had seen. The unimaginable; the moment no Eternal ever considered. One of them was dead; *Rhyma* was dead! Never again would they laugh, or trade insults. Never again would she treat him like the boy he no longer was.

He leapt at the pulsating shape that was once again rearing from the floor: reforming, laughing. A limb, gnarled as an ancient tree, whipped out of the rising shape. It tightened around Elatrynn's throat and raised him, dangling, above the floor.

"Come now, Marudwy," crooned Shilnoth. "We're aware these little mortals you prize so highly indulge in such displays, but must you?" He tittered. "We're practically family, after all! We created your father, which perforce makes us your grandfather."

Elatrynn found it hard to talk past the limb crushing his throat. "That's what makes them so special—" he gasped. "So alive—!"

"Then we see where you get your bad habits." Shilnoth dropped Elatrynn. He turned and glanced through the tall windows, dismissing Elatrynn as worthy of no more thought. Already the growing islands were twice the height of the chamber.

As Elatrynn nursed his raw throat with one hand, he felt something pressed into the other. A sword: Arqyell's sword. The

Inquisitor motioned silence, then gestured at Shilnoth's back. They returned to observing the tableau consuming the Voidal and Uryell.

Elatrynn stared at the sword, then towards the enrapt Shilnoth, who seemed unable to take his eyes off the Islands. The wound dealt by Rhyma still pumped dark fluid. Part of Shilnoth's pulsing shape remained fixed. Uryell had implied both had been injured on Barofonn.

Was Shilnoth weakened? Enough for a sword to end him?

Elatrynn stood, silently and carefully, balancing on the balls of his feet. He had watched Inquisitors many times – observed their ways, their favoured way of moving, their fastest, most efficient sword-strokes. Within reach of Shilnoth, he paused, took a deep, cleansing breath—

"Goodbye, grandfather."

Shilnoth turned as the sword blade cut through his neck. The look of surprise never left his face, even as his tumbling head smacked against a window and rolled back across the floor. Shilnoth's form and feature were stabilised at last.

A shadow fell across the chamber. Elatrynn glanced out of the windows. The risen Islands, now joined in a crude stone caricature of a vast hand, were slowly clenching. The city was about to be crushed.

"Voidal!" Elatrynn knew this had something to do with the Dark Man. But both he and Uryell were still little more than shadows consumed by the Jewel. Were they helping? Had the Jewel trapped them in some way? He looked at Arqyell for guidance, but the Inquisitor looked as helpless as Elatrynn felt.

Then another figure was in the chamber. For a moment Elatrynn thought Rhyma had returned to life, even as he recognised how futile that hope was. The newcomer was dressed in loose black robes, with long white hair and beard. What Elatrynn at first thought was a torch in the man's hand was, he realised, a sword: its sinuous blade burning with golden fire.

The newcomer glanced around the chamber, assessing the situation coolly. "Quickly: gather around the Jewel!" He issued orders as though it was second nature, in a voice belying his apparent age. "Arqyell, stand to the right of the Voidal. You – Elatrynn – stand behind them. I'll take the rear."

Elatrynn was overtaken by the speed of events. "And just who the hell are you—?"

Arqyell was already taking up their position. "Do as he says. Some things begin to make sense, at last."

Too numb to argue further, Elatrynn stood behind the Voidal. Through the windows he could see the rock hand tightening; behind him, he heard the white-haired newcomer chanting. It sounded like a ritual he'd once heard in some far-distant realm, meant to welcome in a new year. But that couldn't be right...

The vast hand contracted further. The chamber roof began to buckle. Chunks of masonry tumbled to the floor, though none ever reached the five clustered by the strobing Jewel. Elatrynn prayed the white-beard knew what he was about. He'd done many irrational things in his day; standing in a collapsing chamber whilst a stranger bade tuneful farewell to an old year was possibly the most foolish.

The Jewel grew more brilliant. It cast rainbow beams which encircled it, lancing through the five figures, linking them. Elatrynn's vision blurred, cleared. He glanced down at his body to see it also flash and glitter like a jewel, shining with an internal furnace. Before him, Uryell, the Voidal and Arqyell burned with the same crystalline inferno. No longer separate entities, they were a multi-limbed creature of sharp facets and harsh light, squatting atop the Nexus Jewel, both shielding and protected by it.

The hand clenched. Piece by piece, the city of Ela'ancidor was crushed. In the Nexus Chamber, the crystalline entity observed the destruction. Accompanied by a clear, high chant, it floated apart from events, witnessing them as distant, inconsequential matters of little importance. Whilst the tiny portion that had been Elatrynn dreamed a dream.

—A dream in which a young Marudwy tears loose from his companions' grasp, and snatches up a fallen crimson ring. It surges, flooding him with blood-red light, drowning his mind in the power of a god. He burns. He screams. He tears at Shilnoth's incoherent shape, ripping it to shreds, banishing him.

—He raises the dying form of his father, once the human Daryed, pouring the Soul Ring back into him. Daryed flares, disperses, flows across the Veilworld. Becoming one with it. Becoming its dead but eternal guardian and barricade—

❦❋❦

THERE WAS NOTHING left on the shores of Bynedd but fine dust. Even the storeys-high hand was gone, the gentle sea once more lapping the Five Islands.

"You may relax now..."

Elatrynn shook his head, dislodging fading memories and dreams. They were five individuals again: dazed and pale, each pair of eyes haunted by what they had witnessed. The pulsing Jewel no longer transfixed the Voidal and Uryell. Indeed, the Jewel itself was gone. Dark Man and Inquisitor stood apart, once more regarding each other variously with dread or suspicion. Arqyell was shaking their head at some private joke.

Elatrynn removed his rapier from the Voidal's unresponsive fingers, unnoticed. He faced the old man and gestured with the sword point. "You're the one." It made a kind of sense, though the reason eluded him. "You brought us here. Why? Who are you?"

A skeletal smile tugged at Arqyell's thin lips. "Can you not guess?"

An apologetic expression fluttered across the old man's face. For a fugitive moment, Elatrynn thought he knew him. "Shilnoth had to be stopped. I couldn't do it alone, and individually, neither could any of you. Uryell had tried alone, and failed – becoming imprisoned for their pains." The green-eyed Inquisitor glared at the old man, who looked away quickly. "Whilst three of us once tried, and failed." His black eyes dulled with painful memories.

At once it became clear. Who else would know so much of Elatrynn's past, and his future. "You're me! An older me—" He faltered, remembering what the old man had done, the magics he'd performed. "And when did I grow so powerful?"

Arqyell laughed harshly. "The ancient you see before us – and I trust you are not fooled by the whitebeard disguise – is the most infuriating Eternal to transverse the Boundless. As you get older, Raven, your passion for experience becomes a positive talent for interfering."

"But you couldn't save Rhyma." Elatrynn's elation at surviving was gone in an instant. He looked around, but could see no sign of her body. "Why...?"

"You know better than to ask," the old man – Raven – said quietly. "We may move through the Boundless with no regard to linearity, yet Time will have the final say. We are none of us immune. Even in Ela'ancidor, what happened is what happened."

Elatrynn sighed. Death was something no well-bred Eternal spoke of: it was the price they all paid for their longevity. Only the gods could escape death, whilst mortals, with their souls, transcended it. Where was the justice? "And the Jewel?"

"Still in Ela'ancidor. It relocated after the Islands rose."

"And this venture you have orchestrated—" Uryell half-raised their staff, pointing it in the old man's direction. "—informing me of Fatecaster's incursion and – I suspect – somehow ensuring I arrived at Barofonn to inform the Shapeless One. To accuse him of the deed, and thus plant the seed upon which he acted...!"

"I had sensed the incursion—"

"Aye – and worked to ensure that Shilnoth would attempt that very act which temporarily breached the Veil, allowing in this—" Uryell angled their staff away from the one called Raven and pointed it at the Voidal.

"A clever and subtle game," said Arqyell, sheathing their sword. "You played your pieces well, Raven. And well for us that you succeeded."

"Was there really any need for us, then?" Elatrynn looked into the

Voidal's blank face. Now it was all over, his part played, it was obvious the man's memory was once again blank. Elatrynn envied him. Perhaps, under the weight of countless memories, oblivion wasn't such a bad prospect after all.

"Of course," said Arqyell when Raven seemed reluctant to answer. "We did what we were fated to do – is that not correct? Beware, Raven – you play the role of god far too well…"

Elatrynn shook his head. "What about Fatecaster?"

"He can return to his own reality," the old man said. "As he speculated, Bynedd may be urged to lap the shores of his Omniverse." He chuckled. "I must voyage there myself."

Arqyell was incredulous. "Even for you that is madness! What sane creature would dare that?" It was clear they included the Voidal.

The Inquisitor Uryell said nothing, but their grim, unforgiving expression spoke eloquently.

Raven glanced at Elatrynn, eyes glittering. "I recall saying, as a younger man, I would give anything to know what lay beyond the Internection. However—" he held up the golden sword: its serpentine blade flickered as though alive "—that's for another day. There is a man to be returned and a breach to be healed."

A distant shape drifted towards them from Bynedd's infinite horizon. Elatrynn stared at it for a while, feeling some of the old man's curiosity, recognising it.

"And what of Rhyma? Is she too returned to Erberow?"

"Of course – for Erberow is life. And she is Erberow. Nothing is lost, my boy…"

"Riddles?"

"An easy one for you to solve." Raven turned to watch the approaching shape.

It resolved into a simple boat, with no sail or oars to propel it. As it neared the shore, Raven urged the Voidal forward. The two Inquisitors regarded it warily, as though the vessel brought with it some contagion.

Elatrynn turned his back on them all: Voidal, Inquisitors, his future self. He snapped his rapier into its sheath and began to walk away. They could all do as they wished, stay or go. For himself, he found he no longer cared.

For now, anyway.

He trudged away from the shore, towards whatever lay beyond the ruins of the city. He would linger in Ela'ancidor a while – this world of yellow grass and lilac skies. Unconsciously as he walked, he reshaped his ragged beard into something trimmed and fine, tailored his worn black clothing into newer, more elegant styles. A broad, plumed hat sat jauntily on his head once more. He paused momentarily, considering. In a second his habitual black was replaced with bright greens, reds and gold. Perhaps it was time to be Marudwy again, if only for a short while. To be himself, to stop fleeing across the Infinite Tiers. Perhaps he would visit Erberow...

And if Ela'ancidor, a Node World, was able to reflect the moods and aspirations of its inhabitants, perhaps he might yet turn that to his advantage.

He walked until the scent of Bynedd was far behind him. Rolling yellow, flecked by black trees, stretched to every horizon. He halted, stabbed his sword into the ground and upon the hilt draped his hat.

With some surprise he realised he was weeping.

He no longer wore a crimson Soul Ring, but a little of its power, its majesty, had stayed within him. He had always felt it. Perhaps, after all, he did have a soul. Or a fragment, at least.

He gazed at the sky, still the same shade of lilac, the great bronze sun hanging immobile. His spirit reached out. Every possibility intersected at a Node World, he touched them all. Worlds where lizard ruled instead of human; worlds where strange flying machines clotted the skies; sterile worlds where life had choked, still-born; worlds where Marudwy – in a multitude of guises – fought against injustice. He touched a world that was hidden from the cosmos; hidden even from itself. A sentient world shielded by an ever-living but dead guardian. He held it close.

"Father...?"

ABOVE THEM THE sky was black, punctuated by dancing lights and glowing shapes. The placid Sea of Bynedd was a perfect mirror: as above, so below. The small boat could have been hanging in space. Despite lacking oars or sail, it still moved effortlessly through the strange waters, leaving no wake or ripple.

Inquisitors Arqyell and Uryell were gone: stepped off onto diverse shores as their spirits had urged them. The *mandra'al* staff lay in the bottom of the boat. Uryell had given it over before departing, their smile uncharacteristically wry. Beside it was the golden sword, Krysolac, the author of much of their recent woes. It embodied a fickle sentience, but it should lead back to where Qrymh and Qryvi had breached the walls of the Boundless, beyond the Wild Precincts.

The Voidal sat in the prow: silent, lost. He was sunken into little more than a fugue state from which he would likely rouse as his own Omniverse neared.

The old man, who was neither old nor a man, sank back against the boat's high stern.

CONTRIBUTORS' NOTES

MIKE CHINN LIVES in Birmingham, UK with his wife Caroline and their tribe of guinea pigs. He's written fiction that runs from Westerns to Sword & Sorcery and Space Opera, via Horror and his British Fantasy Award short-listed Damian Paladin pulp adventure stories (along with its ever expanding universe) to the occasional Sherlock Holmes pastiche, as well as editing four books for The Alchemy Press (*SWORDS AGAINST THE MILLENNIUM*, and *PULP HEROES* volumes one to three). His very first attempts at fiction were a naïve amalgamation of Edgar Rice Burroughs and Michael Moorcock and are, thankfully, lost to posterity.

BORN IN BUENOS Aires, Argentina 1957, Alcatena draws and loves comics – and has been at it for many, many years. His collaborations with Mike Chinn for DC Thomson's *STARBLAZER* are among his favourite stories.

❦ ❦ ❦

ADRIAN COLE IS a native of and lives in North Devon, England. He has had some 3 dozen novels and 200 short stories published over 50 years, working in several genres, including Heroic Fantasy, Sword & Sorcery, Horror, SF, Mythos and supernatural crime. He has appeared in a number of "Year's Best" anthologies and in 2015 his *NICK NIGHTMARE INVESTIGATES* won the prestigious British Fantasy Award for best collection. Recent works include the *WAR ON ROME* saga, the *ELAK OF ATLANTIS* trilogy, a de lux edition reprint of *THE DREAM LORDS* and a dedicated issue of *WEIRDBOOK* Magazine.